For Colin

Thank you for all those cold, wet, muddy trips
to Dufftown and the Cabrach

(And for everything else you do that
makes my writing possible)

Spellchasers
The Beginner's Guide to Curses

LARI DON

Kelpies is an imprint of Floris Books
First published in 2016 by Floris Books

Second printing 2017

The publisher acknowledges subsidy from Creative Scotland towards the publication of this volume

Also available as an eBook

British Library CIP Data available
ISBN 978-178250-305-7
Printed in England by Clays Ltd, St Ives plc

Chapter One

The moment Molly heard the dog growl behind her, she dropped to the ground, low and crouching.

Her world grew wider. She could see almost the whole way round the playing fields without moving her head.

She looked down and saw fur.

On her hands.

Only they weren't hands. They were long brown paws. She twitched. The paws twitched under her.

Oh no, she thought. Not again.

Then she heard the dog louder and closer. Above her, she saw black slavering jaws open wide, yellow teeth ready to snap her spine.

So Molly ran. She ran swift and straight, right across the playing fields. Running faster than she ever thought she could. She had no idea how she was running like this. This incredible fast leaping flight, feet barely touching the ground.

The dog sprinted after her, barking its determination to catch her and rip her and kill her.

Molly ran faster. But the dog was close behind and the hedge at the edge of the playing fields was a long way off.

She was running on instinct. Running because she was being chased. Running because it felt like the right thing to do, with these legs, and this blood pumping through her veins.

But she had no idea what to do next. Would the dog get tired before her? Could she escape if she just kept running?

Then she felt the dog's hot breath on her tail.

Without thinking, Molly switched direction. She leapt to one side and started running parallel to the hedge, away from the straight-line course the dog was struggling to alter.

Her legs had done that. Not her head.

She'd escaped the dog for a moment, but now she wasn't running towards the safety of the hedge.

Molly could see the whole park, all the way around, apart from a narrow blind spot right in front of her nose and another blind spot directly behind her. Her wide field of vision showed the black-and-white hunter hurtling towards her again.

So she ran at amazing grass-skimming speed, dodging towards the hedge, then away, then towards the hedge again.

The dog howled in frustration behind her.

She sprinted and jumped, until at last she reached the hedge and ducked under its lowest branches.

On the other side, Molly tumbled to the ground, landing on her knees and ripping her jeans open.

She gulped a lungful of cold autumn air, glanced at her trembling hands to check they were pale skin, not brown fur, then stood up and looked over the hedge.

A black-and-white greyhound was panting and grinning up at her. Molly gasped and stepped back.

"Oy! Linford!" The man running up behind the dog was red-faced and waving a lead. "Don't worry about him, he won't hurt you. He's had his exercise for today, haven't you, Linford? Did you see them? Did you see how fast they ran?"

"No," said Molly. "Who was running fast?"

"He was chasing a hare! A beautiful long-legged brown hare."

"A hare?"

"Aye, a hare. Like a rabbit but bigger, stronger, smarter and much faster. And it only just got away. Greyhounds were bred to catch hares, and I bet you'd have caught her, yes you would," he rubbed his dog's ears, "you'd have caught her if you'd had a longer run at her."

He smiled at Molly, clipped the lead on the dog's collar and walked off.

"A hare," said Molly again.

So that's what she was. A hare...

Chapter Two

Molly frowned at the headrest of the seat in front of her as they drove through Craigvenie.

Her great-aunt insisted that Molly sat in the back seat, just like when she was little and her mum and dad used to dump her in Speyside for holiday weekends. Molly should probably be grateful she didn't have to squash into the old baby seat she'd seen in the boot when she threw in her overnight bag.

"But why are we going to this farm?"

"Because Aggie Sharpe can help you," said Aunt Doreen, for the fifteenth time that morning.

"But why do you think she can help me? Anyway, I don't need help."

"You do need help, my dear. I don't know exactly what's going on, but I know you shouldn't be screaming yourself awake at night and you shouldn't be ripping so many pairs of jeans either. I wish you'd tell me what's wrong."

Molly didn't say anything.

Doreen snorted. "When we get there, I'll show you why I think Aggie can help."

Molly sighed. She hoped there weren't any dogs on this farm.

Her aunt parked beside a shop in the middle of fields and farm buildings. Molly read the carved wooden sign over the door:

Skene Mains
Farm Shop
– by Craigvenie –
Organic Produce
buy fresh here, or boxes
delivered to your door

Aunt Doreen pushed Molly and her bag into the shop, which was filled with shelves of fruit and herbs, sacks of tatties, boxes of carrots and lots of customers.

Molly wandered towards the lettuces, but Doreen guided her towards the back wall. "Look!"

Molly glanced at leaflets pinned up higgledy piggledy on a cork noticeboard:

The Grimoire Girls:
Book Group meets every Friday

Bendy Babies:
Yoga for little ones

Keep warm this winter!
Knit your own underwear!

"There!" Doreen prodded a faded flyer printed with black and red letters on silver paper:

Curse-Lifting Workshops

All you need to know about lifting curses

- Will work on personal curses, family curses, historical curses
- Guaranteed result
- 5-day course runs during October school holidays every year
- Participants must be between 11 and 21 years old

Residential only, ask at till for details

Molly muttered, "Why would I want a curse-lifting workshop? I'm not *cursed*!"

"Really? When your dad left you here for the tattie holidays, he said you were getting moodier as you got older and I might notice some changes. But he didn't expect you to change *species*, did he? I know you say nothing's wrong, but I remember the old stories and I recognise the signs. So you'll spend the first week of your holidays at Aggie Sharpe's workshop, because I can't send you home to Edinburgh until you're back to normal. Let's check it's not fully booked."

She turned to the till.

"Morning Doreen," said the tall white-haired woman behind the counter. "More grain for your hens?"

Doreen lowered her voice. "I don't need chicken feed today. It's my great-niece. She needs... go on, tell Mrs Sharpe..."

Molly shook her head. She didn't need some old wifey who knitted her own underwear to help her. She didn't need anyone's help. She wasn't cursed. She couldn't be cursed, because curses didn't exist. If she just avoided dogs, everything would be fine.

She tried to back out of the shop, but Aunt Doreen grabbed her arm.

"She needs to do the workshop. You know..." Doreen nodded at the leaflet, "the curse-lifting workshop." She mouthed the words, just breathing the sounds, but Molly was sure everyone in the shop heard.

Mrs Sharpe smiled kindly at Molly. "What's the problem?"

"There is no problem. No problem at all. Thank you very much."

"She annoyed Mr Crottel and she's not been herself since," explained Doreen. "Do you have a spare place on the course?"

Mrs Sharpe frowned. "Mr Crottel. Oh, dear." She looked straight at Molly, staring almost rudely at her face, then at her trembling hands. She nodded. "I can squeeze you in."

"And you guarantee results?" murmured Doreen.

"All the guarantees are in here." Mrs Sharpe lifted a heap of paper from under the counter. "Do you want to read it now?"

Doreen fumbled her glasses out of her handbag and peered at the small print. "I'll take your word for it, Aggie. And there's no need to fill in a form." Doreen swung Molly behind the counter. "Here she is. She's Molly Drummond, she's eleven years old and I'll be back for her at the end of the week." Then she rushed out of the shop.

Molly turned to Mrs Sharpe. "I'm not cursed," she whispered.

"Let's not quibble about wording, my dear, spells and enchantments are covered too. I'm busy in the shop just now, so go round to the barn yourself. Out this back door, turn right, head for the red door. Your classmates are already there. Go in and introduce yourself. Don't be shy."

"I'm not shy," muttered Molly. "And I'm not cursed..."

But all the customers were staring at her, leeks and

apples and parsley in their hands, so she muttered thanks to the old lady and pushed out through the back door.

There was a wooden building to her right. She walked towards it, opened the red door and stepped inside.

Molly walked into a cold barn filled with wooden desks and chairs. She saw a tall wide-shouldered boy with very short blond hair leaning against an old-fashioned blackboard. Standing in front of the boy, scowling at him, was a slim girl with a cloud of suspiciously purple hair. They broke off their argument to stare at Molly.

Molly pushed her own short brown hair behind her ears, took another step inside and pulled the door behind her.

"Don't stand on the toad!" yelled the girl.

Molly looked down. There was a sand-coloured frog in front of her. At least, it looked like a frog. But maybe the purple-haired girl was an expert on amphibians and it was actually a toad.

"We don't know the toad's name," said the boy. "But presumably you can tell us yours."

"I'm Molly Drummond and I don't think I'm in the right place."

"Did Mrs Sharpe send you here?" he asked.

Molly nodded reluctantly.

"Then you're in the right place."

Molly didn't want this to be the right place, so she shook her head.

"Are you looking for a different course?" the boy asked. "Nurture your own bread dough was last week and next week is..."

"Knit your own underwear," said Molly, trying not to smile.

He grinned. "Yes. But this week is curse lifting. *We're* both in the right place." He gestured to the girl and himself. "And I assume the toad is in the right place. If you're sure you're in the wrong place, you'd better go back to the shop and buy some cabbages."

He turned to the girl. "And you're wrong about Mrs Sharpe—"

"Hold on," interrupted Molly. "You're actually here for a curse-lifting workshop?"

"Of course," said the girl. "Mrs Sharpe only runs it once a year. I've been waiting all my life to be old enough to do it."

Molly looked at the boy, who had the right number of arms and legs, and was dressed in an ordinary white shirt and jeans. She looked at the girl, who was pale and pretty and Goth-looking, with her purple hair, droopy black clothes and silver jewellery. Neither of them seemed particularly odd or obviously magical.

"But..." Molly hesitated. "But are you both cursed?"

The girl nodded. "Aren't you?"

"Of course not. I don't believe in curses or spells or magic or frogs turning into princes. I'm not cursed,"

she said, so firmly she almost convinced herself, "and I'm not staying..."

Then a cat walked out from behind a desk.

A big black cat.

A huge black cat, its head higher than Molly's waist.

But it wasn't a cat. It couldn't be a cat. Because it had narrow black wings folded over its back and a long-nosed, elegant, almost-human face.

The black creature walked right towards Molly.

Molly sat down, very fast, on the floor. Almost landing on the toad.

The girl with the bushy purple hair picked the toad up and placed it on a desk. "You'll be safer there."

Then the boy and the girl grabbed an arm each, pulled Molly up and sat her on a wobbly school chair.

The not-quite-cat sat down neatly in front of Molly, opened its human mouth and spoke in a soft deep voice. "This week, you'll have to believe in curses and spells and magic. My name is Atacama and I'm delighted to make your acquaintance."

Molly took a deep breath. "Pleased to meet you too, Atacama."

The girl perched on the wooden desk opposite Molly. "I'm Beth and I'm here because my family has been cursed for years. Atacama is here because he was cursed last week. And this is—"

"I can introduce myself, thank you," said the boy. "I'm Innes and my brother was killed by a curse last year.

I'm here to lift the curse before it kills me and the rest of my family too. Atacama, Beth and I are neighbours, we all live in or near the local tributaries of the River Spey. But we've never met the toad before, and we've never met you. So why are you here, Molly?"

"I don't know. I'm not cursed." She sighed. If she wasn't cursed, what was happening to her?

Innes frowned. "Did Mrs Sharpe accept you on the workshop?"

Molly nodded.

"Then she thinks you've been cursed and she thinks it can be lifted. So you'd better admit that to yourself." He smiled. "Then tell us all about it."

Molly shook her head.

Beth scowled at Innes. "Stop trying to make friends with her. Just let her leave. If she doesn't believe in curses or spells, she'll make this workshop *impossible.* If we waste days waiting for her to admit curses exist, then days studying 'Curses for Babies', we won't have time to learn any complex curse lore by the end of the week, and we might not get our own curses lifted."

Innes shrugged. "So let's teach her the ABC of curses ourselves, then Mrs Sharpe won't have to."

Atacama nodded. "If we share our basic knowledge with the human girl this afternoon, we'll all be better prepared for whatever wisdom the witch plans to teach us this evening."

Molly was still struggling to concentrate on the mean-

ing of any words coming out of the winged black cat's human mouth, but she heard one of them loud and clear.

"The witch? Mrs Sharpe is a witch?"

Chapter Three

"Of course I'm a witch." Mrs Sharpe's wrinkled face appeared round the edge of the red door. "That's why I run grimoire book groups and teach curse-lifting workshops. That's why my herbal teabags are famous all over Speyside."

"But what about the underwear knitting workshops?" asked Molly.

"Everyone needs to keep warm in winter, my dear. Even witches. So, have you all made friends?"

Beth snorted, and Atacama said, "We're getting to know Molly, but we haven't had time to chat to the toad."

"The toad? I don't have a toad on the register." Mrs Sharpe looked at the large warty amphibian squatting on the desk. "We can get you signed up later."

"Are we starting now?" Innes sat down, opened a notebook and held up a sharp pencil.

"Not yet. The first lesson will be tonight, after the last customer has left. In the meantime, you can howk the tatties out of the narrow field."

"We're here to learn, not to work," muttered Beth.

"You can consider your curses while you dig, and if you work until you're bone-tired and a bit sorry for yourselves, you'll be in the right frame of mind for learning tonight. I've put forks, buckets and wellies outside the door, so get started."

Mrs Sharpe nodded to them and shut the door behind her. The door closed smoothly and quietly, not creakily and spookily like Molly would have expected a witch's door to sound.

Beth sighed. "That's what I was trying to tell you, Innes. She holds this workshop in October to get free labour at harvest time. She told my uncle that because students can think about curses and dig at the same time, it's easier to get her tatties lifted by this workshop than by the bread-making or sew your own teabag ones. But I don't want to be slave labour for a witch!"

Innes rolled up his sleeves. "I don't mind giving her a hand. Every single being who does this workshop goes home without their curse. I'll happily dig all her fields if I can lift the curse on my family. Come on, everyone..."

Molly was bending down in a muddy field, wearing someone else's flappy wellies, digging up potatoes with a fork and dropping them in a red bucket.

She straightened up, stretched the kinks out of her spine and looked around.

She knew the toad was somewhere nearby. When they'd arrived in the field, Beth had reminded them to keep an eye out so they didn't stand on the toad or drive a fork into it. Then the toad had started digging, slower than the rest of them, but still working hard. The toad had also surprised Molly by walking from each plant to the next in a sprawly sort of crawl, rather than hopping.

Molly had moved along ten ridged rows of tatties since then, so she'd no idea where the toad was now.

She could see Innes and Beth to her left, both loosening the earth round the tattie shaws then howking up the roots, pulling off the pale tubers and dropping them into the nearest bucket. Innes had suggested they all work close together. He claimed they would work faster if they didn't get too far apart. And though it was hard work, they were moving across the field at an impressive speed.

Atacama was over to Molly's right, looking like a large cat scratching in a huge litter tray. He'd offered to loosen the potato plants a row ahead, so those with hands to hold forks had less work to do. Molly said 'Thanks' to him every time she moved to a new row, but she didn't mention the litter tray comparison. Atacama was too dignified, and his claws were too sharp, for that to be a kind or sensible thing to say.

Molly stretched her arms up to ease her aching muscles. She said, "Aren't scarecrows meant to *scare* crows?"

She pointed at half a dozen ragged black birds perched on the stick arms and turnip head of a scarecrow in the next field.

"The farmer has to move them around and change their clothes regularly for the crows to stay scared of them," said Beth, picking earth from under her silver-painted nails.

"If we're going to chat rather than dig, let's talk about something useful," said Innes. "Let's give Molly the beginner's guide to curses now, so Mrs Sharpe doesn't have to run through it tonight."

Molly sighed. "But I'm not cursed..."

"We can't teach her about curses if she refuses to accept they exist," said Beth, "so don't waste your breath on her, Innes. Just keep digging."

Molly wondered if the best way to deal with Beth's constant rudeness was to ignore it. She turned her back on Beth and pulled another handful of tatties from the earth. They looked so fresh and crunchy, and it had been a long time since breakfast in Aunt Doreen's kitchen. Molly often ate raw carrot and raw turnip. Perhaps she could eat raw potato?

"Do we get fed meals here or do we just eat the vegetables we dig up?"

"I think that's our tea over there," Beth waved her fork towards a big basket at the other side of the field. Molly didn't think it had been there when they arrived.

"We shouldn't eat until we've finished the whole field," said Innes.

"Are you the witch's factor or foreman or something?" demanded Beth.

"I'm just being practical, giving us an incentive."

Beth muttered something about teacher's pets and bent back down to the tatties.

They scratched and dug and howked for another half hour, getting stiffer and muddier and sweatier as they worked their way across the field.

Molly occasionally heard noises from the carpark by the shop. Doors slamming, babies wailing, car engines revving. And the crows on the scarecrow sometimes cawed. But the tattie-diggers worked in silence.

Eventually, Innes stood up straight and dropped his fork on the ground. "Let's just tell her what we all are, then see if she'll admit her own curse. Even if it doesn't work, at least it will pass the time."

"There are other ways to pass the time," said Beth, stepping over to a ridge where the toad was loosening a clod of earth. "Atacama could ask us riddles, for example."

Atacama growled at her, showing teeth as long and sharp as his claws. Molly took a step back, but Beth just laughed.

Then Molly thought about riddles and deserts and cats with human faces, and smiled. She'd read a lot of books; perhaps she wasn't a complete beginner after all.

Innes rubbed earth off his hands. "Curses are nothing to be ashamed of, Molly. I'm here to lift a curse that was cast on my father, not on me. But it's a curse that affects my whole family and all the running water in the Spey valley. It's a curse that stops me and my family hunting underwater in our rivers any time the moon is in the sky, and it's a curse that will kill us if we aren't careful."

Molly stared at him. She had no idea what he was talking about and no idea how she should respond.

Beth laughed. "Unless you tell her what you are, Innes, talking about rivers and hunting won't have the dramatic impact you're hoping for!"

Innes shrugged. "If she was any kind of worthwhile human, she'd already have guessed what I am."

"She hasn't a clue. Perhaps your family aren't as famous and recognisable as you think!"

Innes turned to Molly, "Are you one of those humans who's completely blind to the magic all around you? If you don't know what I am, or what Beth is, or what Atacama is, then you're missing out on half the world."

Beth said, "Give up, Innes. She didn't know Mrs Sharpe was a witch, and that's obvious to almost everyone in Craigvenie, so she's never going to guess what the rest of us are."

"But I do know what Atacama is," said Molly. "You're a sphinx, aren't you? You're named after a desert and you're an expert on riddles, so you're a sphinx."

Atacama nodded. "I am a sphinx. But I'm not an expert on riddles any more, because I've lost my own riddle."

"Oh, I'm sorry," said Molly. "How did you lose it?"

"Like all of us, I'm the victim of a dark spell commonly

known as a curse. I was guarding a door, and I refused admission to a being who couldn't answer my riddle. He cursed me so that I can remember the answer to my riddle, but I can't remember the question. Until I can remove that magical barrier from my memory, I'm not a true sphinx, so I can't guard anything. I might as well dig fields." He looked down and swiped at the earth with one wide paw. The toad jumped out of the way.

Atacama looked so sad that, before she could stop herself, Molly reached out and laid her hand between his pointed black ears. His fur was soft and warm, and as she stroked it gently, Atacama's long smooth face moved into an awkward smile. "Thank you for your concern."

Molly patted his head and removed her hand.

Innes said, "So you can recognise a sphinx when you see his face and his wings and someone says 'riddle' right in front of you. Well done – you obviously read the right books. What about me and Beth? What are we?"

Molly stared at them, standing side by side, looking as un-magical as any of her friends in Edinburgh. She shrugged.

"Would you like a clue, perhaps?" murmured Atacama.

Molly smiled at the sphinx. "Yes, please."

Beth shook her head. "That's cheating. If humans can't recognise what we are without help, they don't deserve to know."

Innes nodded. "Usually I'd agree with you, but I like

the idea of clues. It might give Atacama back his riddling confidence and help us work out how ignorant Molly really is."

"Actually, I do know what you all are," said Molly. "You're all rude. Apparently, I don't deserve to know," she glared at Beth, "and I'm ignorant," she glared at Innes. "Is everyone in your world this unfriendly?"

"I'm not trying to be unfriendly, just practical," said Beth. "So, a clue about each of us, then try to guess what we are. If you guess right, maybe we'll help you with homework and coursework. If you guess wrong, you're on your own."

Innes said, "No, that's too hard. Let's allow her to ask three questions as well, with one-word answers. A riddle then three questions, so we can find out what she knows and how she thinks." He looked at Molly. "Beth is right. This workshop is too important for us to waste our time helping someone with no knowledge of magic. But she's wrong too. I don't think abandoning you will do us any good. Mrs Sharpe wants us in the right frame of mind to lift our curses, and I don't think treading everyone else underfoot is the best way to get there. So we'll give you a fair chance. If you succeed, it will prove you have a feel for magic, and we'll make you part of our team. But if you fail, it will prove you have so little sense of our world that you'll probably never lift your curse anyway, and you might as well sit in the corner for the week rather than slow us down. Are you up for the challenge?"

Molly remembered her speed as a hare running over the playing fields. "I bet I'm faster than any of you, so I don't think I will slow you down. But if I have to spend this week doing a workshop about magic I don't believe in, and digging vegetables I'm not going to eat, then I suppose I'd rather be in a team – even with you lot – than on my own. I'll try to guess what you are, and if I fail, I won't expect any help at all."

Chapter Four

Molly stepped backwards over a ridge of undug tatties and looked at her fellow diggers. The toad was squatting by a discarded fork, Beth and Innes were standing together by a red bucket, Atacama was sitting tidily in front of them.

"I'm ready," she said.

Atacama spoke, in a formal chanting voice:

Innes shifts shape even faster than he runs,
And when he runs fast on four legs,
Then you should fear him.

Molly gasped. Not because she was meant to fear Innes, but because Innes changed shape, like she did, which meant she had lots of questions she needed to ask him. But she could only ask three questions right now, so she had to choose carefully.

Molly thought about the collections of myths and legends on the magical shelves in the school library, where she'd first read about sphinxes and their riddles. "Innes,

I don't think you're in the same myth books as Atacama's family. Would I find you in stories from colder places?"

"That's right. Colder *wetter* places."

"One-word answers only," snapped Beth. "Don't help her."

Molly couldn't let the purple-haired girl's antagonism distract her. She kept looking at Innes when she asked, "When you change shape to something four-legged, are you furry or slimy or scaly?"

He frowned. "How do I answer that in one word? Hair. That's the one word."

"Hare! You're a hare?"

"No! Hair, like..." He ran the palm of his hand over his short blond hair. "Hair and mane and tail..."

"*One* word, Innes."

"But she has to understand the one word and 'hair' is confusing when it's not written down."

Molly was smiling now. She thought she knew the answer, but she still had one more question. "Do you keep your hair short so it doesn't have waterweed tangled in it when you come out of the water onto the land?"

He grinned. "Yes I do! Well done..."

"She still has to say it," said Beth. "What is he? Exactly?"

"He's a water-horse, a kelpie, a shapeshifter who can be a horse or human on land, and a monster in the water. Oh sorry, Innes! Maybe monster is the wrong word? Maybe you're something really gentle and cute underwater?"

"No, monster is just about right. And, yes, I'm a kelpie. Good for you!"

“So have you been cursed to become a kelpie?” asked Molly.

“No...” Innes answered. “My ancestors have always been kelpies. We’re proud to be kelpies. But our curse is nothing to be proud of.”

“Oh, sorry.” Molly remembered another detail from those old Scottish stories: children going missing by lochs. “But... don’t kelpies eat people?”

“Sometimes. There’s a picnic over there, though, so you’re safe until well after tea-time.” He smiled at her, but she didn’t manage to smile back.

Beth said, “Kelpies are easy to guess. Kelpies are show-offs, so everyone knows about kelpies. What am I?”

Molly looked at Beth’s purple hair, pale face and stylish dark clothes. “A rock star?”

Innes laughed. “She might dress like it, but she’s not a fan of rocks. Beth is more botany than geology.”

“Shut up! Don’t give her clues. That’s Atacama’s job.”

Atacama nodded and spoke in his calm deep voice:

If Innes is wet, then Beth is dry,
And while his kind drown and eat yours,
Your kind slice and burn hers.

Molly frowned. “Do we? I only slice bread and cheese. Don’t answer! That wasn’t one of my questions!”

Beth scowled at her, but didn’t answer.

Molly thought about the burning and the black clothes.

"Are you a witch?"

"NO! That's my one-word answer, and my comment is: how dare you think I'm a witch? Witches are humans with a bit of magic. I am not human and I wouldn't want to be. And I would *never* want to be a nasty cruel dangerous witch. If your next question is that insulting, I won't even answer it!"

"Sorry, I didn't realise it was an insult. Mrs Sharpe seems like a very nice witch."

"She's alright, for a witch. But most witches use their spells to cause immense amounts of trouble for everyone and everything around them."

"If you can't manage one-word answers, perhaps one sentence is enough," said Innes, with a grin.

Molly noticed, for the first time, Beth's long narrow hands and spring-green eyes. And she looked more closely at that messy cloud of purple hair.

She blurted out: "Do you dye your hair purple, or is that colour natural?"

"It's natural," said Beth, clipped and short and very uninformative.

Molly only had one question left, and she wasn't any closer to knowing what Beth was. She definitely wasn't a witch. And she wasn't a water creature either, because the riddle said she was dry.

Molly repeated Atacama's riddle, and Beth winced at the last few words.

So Molly asked, "When my people slice your people –

which I'm sorry about, by the way – what do they use? A sword, a carving knife, a lawnmower, an axe, a laser, what?"

Beth whispered, "An axe. Or a saw."

Molly remembered Innes's joke about geology and botany. She was fairly sure that botany was the study of plants.

"Oh! You're a—"

"Careful!" said Innes. "Careful. You have to say the correct word. We've given you a lot of leeway, but you have to get this exactly right."

"But I don't know how to get it exactly right!" Molly's head was filling up with words like nymph and naiad and dryad and neried and woodsprite… But she had no idea which one was the perfect word.

Molly didn't want to get this wrong. However fast she could run, she couldn't keep up with these people in a classroom, because she knew nothing about magic and spells. If they didn't help her, she'd be left behind, always chasing after them. Then she'd be stuck with this curse, if that's what it was, for the rest of her life.

She sighed. "I don't know. I'm sorry. I don't know the exact word for what you are, Beth, but I can describe it. Can I do that instead?"

Beth glanced at Innes and Atacama, then nodded.

"You're the spirit of a tree. I even know which tree. My favourite tree, because it's such an amazing colour in the winter. With black-and-silver bark, and a cloud of purply brown twigs. I think you're the spirit of a silver birch tree. Am I right?"

"You're wrong," said Innes, slowly. "She's not the spirit of *one* silver birch, but *all* the silver birches in one wood. Not one tree, but many."

"You're nearly right. That's good enough," said Beth. "Are silver birches really your favourite tree?"

Molly nodded. "Even now I know birches are really rude in person, they're still the most beautiful trees in the world."

Beth frowned. "I'm not always rude, just when I'm scared that someone is going to prevent me saving my trees by risking the success of this workshop."

"So, what is the word, then?" Molly asked. "Is it woodsprite or naiad or— Hold on! Atacama's riddle said that Innes is wet and you're dry. Are you a dryad?"

Beth nodded.

"But aren't you meant to be all floaty and made of pretty flowers and leaves?"

"No, I'm a tree spirit, not a flower fairy. I'm as hard as wood and as strong as a tree trunk."

"Yeah, you don't mess with a dryad," said Innes. "So now we're a team, Molly, tell us about your curse."

Molly picked up her fork and stepped carefully round the toad. She started to loosen the earth round another tattie shaw. "Maybe after we've eaten."

Now Molly knew that her classmates were all properly magical. A shapeshifter. A tree spirit. A mythical riddling sphinx. The toad was probably a prince. Their curses were probably cast by evil wizards with impressive cloaks, because of important magical disagreements.

Molly, however, just changed into a small brown rabbity thing. Even if she could admit she'd been cursed, she knew she couldn't admit what she'd been arguing about when it happened, or what had been all over her shoe.

Innes sighed. "Ok, keep it to yourself if you want. Everyone else, get digging, while I run through a quick ABC of curses for the girl of mystery here."

Beth said, "I hope you can talk and dig at the same time. You need to work beside us if we're going to keep up this speed. You start and I'll interrupt when you get things wrong..."

Molly smiled. She wasn't going to learn much from this pair unless they stopped arguing.

Then Atacama said, in his calm formal voice, "There are several ways to find yourself under a curse. You can be cursed as a specific individual like I was, or you can inherit a curse like Beth, or be endangered by someone else's curse like Innes. Is yours a personal curse or a family one, Molly?"

She muttered, "It's just me."

"There are new curses and historical curses. Beth has a very old curse, several centuries old. Innes's curse is almost a year old, and mine was cast last week. How fresh is your curse, Molly?"

She sighed. "Just a couple of days."

"There are curses cast by the living, where the curse-caster is still available to negotiate with, and there are dying curses, which can be especially strong. Were you cursed by someone's last breath?"

Molly wondered if she should just tell the whole story now, rather drip it out in bits and pieces in response to Atacama's polite questions.

Then she heard a car door slam, and a voice shout, "No, Tilly! Come back!"

And she heard a dog bark.

Molly felt a familiar flash of heat along her spine.

She dropped to the ground, low and crouching...

She saw the big cat looming over her and a flock of birds circling high above. She heard the dog bark closer, and she felt very small and very tasty.

So Molly started to run.

Chapter Five

Molly leapt over the earth she'd just been digging.

She heard the dog bark again, and zigzagged as she sprinted away. She saw it to her left, hairy and golden, bouncing cheerfully and hungrily towards her. It probably didn't have the speed of a greyhound, but it would still happily savage her if she made a mistake and let it catch up.

The earth wasn't as smooth and easy on her paws as grass. And there wasn't a fence or a hedge nearby, just high stone walls. Molly knew how far she could leap forwards as a hare, but she'd no idea if she could do the high jump.

She hurtled round the field, searching for a way out. But she couldn't see a gate. She still wasn't completely used to the blind spot in front of her nose and she couldn't stop moving to look properly.

She heard shouting behind her. An adult voice, in the distance, yelling for Tilly to come back. Then Beth and Innes, nearer, yelling at the dog to go away.

Molly could see Beth standing white-faced in the middle of the field, with Atacama crouched at her feet. She didn't run towards them, because this wasn't the time to find out what sphinxes liked to eat.

Molly felt trapped. She could run like this for ages, but she needed somewhere to run towards.

She saw the dog behind her right shoulder. It was running straight for her, and she still had no idea how to get away. She switched direction again, dashing to her left.

And she saw a gate, at the top corner of the field.

Molly ran towards the gap under the wooden bars. In a few more bounds, she darted under it, fitting easily through the space between wood and earth.

She ran across a field of undug tatties, feeling a sudden desire to lie down, keep still and hope the dog wouldn't see her. But that would be too risky, because she could already hear the dog's bark of triumph as it squeezed under the gate and started chasing again.

Molly sprinted towards the other side of the field, hoping for another gate with a lower bottom plank this time.

But when she reached the other side, there was no gate.

She suddenly realised this must be the last field on Mrs Sharpe's farm. There was no gate because this was the limit of her land. And this boundary wall was higher than the walls between Mrs Sharpe's own fields. It looked too high to jump.

The golden dog was already halfway across the field.

And it wasn't the only thing following her.

Now there was a horse following her too. A big white horse, huge hooves churning up the earth, crashing onto the ground like an earthquake.

The horse was chasing the dog.

The dog was chasing the hare.

And the hare had nowhere to go.

Molly ran frantically along the base of the wall, hoping for a hidden gate or a few tumbledown stones.

She heard a squeal behind her. The horse had caught up with the dog and was slashing at the dog with its teeth. Molly watched, shocked into stillness, as the horse bit down.

The horse snapped its mouth shut just above the dog's ears. It had missed deliberately. But the dog didn't know that; it howled and ran off.

The horse galloped towards Molly.

Molly wondered if the white horse was a kelpie, if the white horse was Innes, and remembered Atacama saying she should fear him when he ran fast on four legs.

She sprinted up the edge of the field, still hoping for a gap in the wall.

But there was no gap, and the huge horse was almost on top of her.

So Molly swivelled round, took a run at the wall and...

Jumped.

She cleared the top stones with ease.

On the other side, Molly fell awkwardly on her human

hip and shoulder, and only just rolled out of the way as the white horse landed elegantly beside her.

Before she could scramble to her feet and run off, the horse was already a boy.

"Wow!" Innes reached out a hand to pull her up. "You're fast! Fast and tricky!"

She ignored the hand and used the rough stones of the wall to pull herself up.

"But what's with all the dodging about and zigzagging?" Innes asked. "Surely it means you have to run further? I just choose a spot and gallop straight at it."

Molly said, "Are you being hunted when you gallop?"

"Not usually, no."

"I think the dodging is to throw off pursuit, and anyway I didn't have a spot to run towards, because I couldn't see a gate."

"You didn't need a gate! You cleared the wall with loads to spare. You're a serious athlete in that hare form. I'd love to race you to find out who's faster, a stallion or a hare."

Molly clambered over the wall. "But aren't you most dangerous when you're four-legged?"

"Not to hares. Too much fur, not enough meat, all those small bones are a choking hazard. You don't need to worry about me when you're a hare!"

As they walked across the undug tattie field, Molly asked, "So how do you do that? How do *we* do that?"

"Do what?"

"Change. Into a horse. Or a hare. How is it possible to

change into something so much bigger than you, or so much smaller than me?"

She looked at the hare's prints in the earth as she covered them with the soles of her wellies. Long leaps, but small paws. The hare must be a tiny fraction of her human size.

"Have you done physics at school yet?" asked Innes.

"No, I'm not in S1 until next year."

"Me neither, but my dad explained it to me. There are huge gaps between all the different bits of an atom. The nucleus is like the sun, and the electrons are like orbiting planets, with vast spaces in between. We look solid and we feel solid. So do Beth's trees, the water in the river, the stones of that wall. But actually we're mostly made up of gaps between the atoms and gaps within the atoms. So Dad thinks shapeshifting expands or squeezes those gaps. It also moves the atoms around into slightly different, but not completely different, formations. I can shift into a fish or a horse, but not a stone or a tree, because all animals are built from the same basic proteins."

Molly frowned. "But you definitely weigh more as a horse, I heard you thunder across that field. And I weigh less as a hare, because I couldn't leap like that if I didn't. How does science explain that?"

"No idea." Innes grinned. "I might explain it better when I've passed Higher Physics and Biology!"

"So you go to school?"

"Of course. So does Beth."

"Do your classmates know what you are?"

"Not all of them, just ones from families who tell the old stories. But no one really minds kelpies, so long as we don't eat their children."

"And do you?"

"Not if someone provides me with regular picnics," replied Innes, as he climbed over the gate. Which by Molly's count was the third time he hadn't answered that question properly.

As they walked across the field towards Beth and the others, Molly said quietly, "Thanks."

"For what?"

"For scaring off the dog."

"No problem. You're so fast I'm sure you'd have got away yourself, but I was happy to help. We're a team, aren't we?"

Innes walked past Beth and sat down by the basket. "I'm hungry. Let's eat."

Beth said, "Oh, now *you're* hungry, so it's time to eat."

Molly said, "I'd prefer he ate too."

Beth nodded. "Let's eat, then finish digging."

Innes found wipes and water in the basket, which they used to clean earth off their hands and paws. Then he passed out rolls to those with hands, and a roast chicken for the one with paws.

Beth looked at the toad. "Mrs Sharpe didn't pack for you, because you're not on the register. Would you like my salad?" She pulled a lettuce leaf out of her cheese roll and placed it in front of the toad.

Then she said, "So, now we know. Molly is a part-time hare. How did that happen?"

"What's the trigger?" asked Innes.

"How do you turn back?" asked Atacama.

Molly sighed. "I should just tell you the whole story. But it's a bit embarrassing."

Innes laughed. "Curses aren't usually good-behaviour prizes. Most of them have embarrassing or unflattering or even criminal stories behind them. Just tell us what happened."

So Molly told them:

"I'm staying with my Aunt Doreen for the October holidays. Doreen Drummond, she lives on the corner opposite the big distillery. The first morning I was here, I was walking past her neighbour's house and I trod in a pile of dog dirt. I realised the pavement was covered in little stinky piles, it was like doing the slalom on the ski slope getting round them all. I asked Aunt Doreen if that stretch of pavement was some kind of local dog toilet, and she said no, but Mr Crottel is lazy and throws his own dogs' mess out of his garden onto the pavement, rather than cleaning it up properly. But, she said, don't mention it to him, because he can get quite grumpy.

"That afternoon, I was walking on the road to avoid the disgusting heaps on the pavement, and he threw dog dirt over the hedge and it *hit me.* It actually hit me. On the leg. It splattered against my jeans and slid down onto my trainers. So I shouted at him. He shouted back. It became a bit of an argument. Then he waved his hands about and used really old-fashioned language I didn't completely understand, and now...

"Well, now every time I hear a dog bark or growl, I turn into a hare. I didn't even know what I was turning into the first few times. It was... it was quite scary..." Her voice tailed off as she remembered the first time.

"I bet it was," said Innes. "Kelpies aren't allowed to shift until we're seven years old, and even then we have our whole family around us to stop us panicking."

"How did you work out what you were?" Beth asked Molly. "Did you examine your pawprints?"

"I didn't think of that. I found out when a dog owner told me what animal he'd seen his dog chasing."

"Hares are wise and tricky animals, as well as fast," said Atacama. "If Mr Crottel transformed you into a hare deliberately, he knew you wouldn't be easy to catch. He may not have intended it to be a fatal curse."

"I think he wanted to give the local dogs sport, rather than give me a sporting chance, judging by what he yelled at me."

"Is it only dogs that trigger the shift? Not other predators?" Beth asked.

Molly shrugged. "Atacama looks like a panther, like those big cats people sometimes report sightings of round here..."

Atacama sighed. "We can't stay hidden all the time."

"So you look like a predator, but even when I got a

surprise meeting you in the classroom, I didn't turn into a hare. And birds flying overhead," she glanced round at the scarecrow, "like those crows, or even hawks, don't make me change either. I think it's just dogs. Which makes sense, if any of it makes sense at all, because it was dogs we argued about."

"What shifts you back?" asked Innes.

"I don't know. I run for ages, then change back when I least expect it."

"Tell us exactly where you've changed, every time," said Atacama.

"The first time, I changed back to a girl when I ran across a road. That was a bit awkward. The second time, I made it into someone's garden under a fence. Yesterday, I reached the edge of the playing field and pushed through a hedge, and just now when I jumped the wall. Perhaps I turn back when I cross from one field or space to another?"

"It can't be that simple," said Atacama. "You didn't shift back when you went under the gate between the fields."

"Oh. No. Maybe we can figure it out during the workshop. Though if Mrs Sharpe can lift the curse before I meet any more dogs, I won't need to find out what turns me back to a girl, because I'll never become a hare again."

Chapter Six

After they'd dug up all the potatoes in the small field and dragged the buckets to the back of the shop, they collapsed into chairs in the chilly classroom.

Mrs Sharpe walked through the red door, clean, smiling and smelling of fresh herbs. She nodded at everyone slumped, muddy and exhausted, at their desks. "I see the buckets are full of tatties. You did the narrow field so fast, I'm sure you'll manage a bigger field tomorrow. Now, are you ready to start some *serious* digging?"

Beth sighed. "Not more digging."

"This is digging with words rather than forks. How much do you know about your own curses?"

Before anyone could answer, Mrs Sharpe started writing on the blackboard in clear blocky letters that Molly recognised from the price boards in the shop. But the prices of cauliflower and kale were written in white chalk; these words were written in bright red chalk.

Innes opened his notebook and carefully copied the witch's words down.

Molly looked round for pen and paper, but Beth, sitting behind her, whispered, "Don't worry, Innes will get it all. We can borrow his notes if we need to." So Molly leant back and watched the witch write questions:

- WHO CAST THE CURSE?
- WHEN WAS THE CURSE CAST?
- WHY WAS THE CURSE CAST?
- WAS THE CURSE JUSTIFIED AND REASONABLE, OR DISPROPORTIONATE?
- WAS IT A DYING CURSE?
- ARE THERE LIMITS TO THE CURSE?
- DOES THE CURSE SPECIFY A TASK OR QUEST THAT WILL LIFT THE CURSE?
- IS THE CURSE-CASTER STILL LIVING?
- WOULD AN APOLOGY HELP?
- WHAT WOULD YOU SACRIFICE TO BE FREE OF THIS CURSE?

Innes was scribbling fast, Atacama was staring at the moving chalk like a cat watching a bird, the toad was squatting on a desk, and Beth was slouching in her chair.

Then Mrs Sharpe wrote one last question:

- DO YOU DESERVE TO BE FREE OF THIS CURSE?

She turned round. "Anyone know the answers to all these questions?"

There was silence. Not even Atacama knew *everything*.

"We can't answer that last one ourselves, can we?" Molly said, eventually. "Surely someone else would have to decide if we deserved our curse. Is there a curse court or exam board or something? A judge who decides if people deserve their curses? Do we have to sit a test to lift these curses?"

Mrs Sharpe shook her head. "It's not like learning to drive or getting your cycling proficiency. And the wider world of curses is too advanced for this workshop." She frowned as the toad knocked a pencil off its desk and the pencil rolled noisily across the floor.

"But Molly is right: the last question is different. You can't answer it until you know the answers to the others.

"So your homework for tomorrow is to find answers to all these questions, ideally by interviewing the person who knows most about your curse. Then bring the answers back to the farm and share them with your fellow classmates. I also expect you to harvest the tatties from the field nearest the farmhouse before the sun sets again. I'll see you here this time tomorrow evening to set you another task."

"But..." said Molly.

"Yes, my dear?"

"But... the only person who can answer those questions is the man who cursed me."

Mrs Sharpe walked over to a wall of wooden cupboards, each door stencilled with the name of a different workshop. She pulled a few sheets of paper out of the cupboard marked:

CURSE-LIFTING WORKSHOP SUPPLIES

and handed them to Molly.

"So you'd better visit your curse-caster. He might even lift your curse, if you ask nicely. But it's not wise to bother dark-magic users when there is no light in the sky. You should all go to bed soon, then wake early to dig up my tatties – and dig up your curses."

Molly looked at the top sheet. It was printed with the questions Mrs Sharpe had written on the board and spaces to fill in the answers.

Mrs Sharpe said, "One more piece of health-and-safety advice. It can be risky to speak to dark-magic practitioners even in daylight, so I suggest you go in teams."

The door closed behind her.

"I told you she was into teamwork," said Innes. "There are five of us, so that's a team of two and a team of three. Beth, you'd better take Molly"

"Why? Because she's a girl? We're not going shopping for makeup, you know."

"Not because she's a girl, because your family history isn't full of eating people."

"Our family history is full of humans cutting our trees down."

"I can go on my own," Molly said, as she handed out

the sheets of paper. "Or with Atacama, or the toad..." She glanced at the toad, then added, "Couldn't we just lift the toad's curse right now? You know, with a kiss?"

They all stared at the toad. The shiny, warty, pale brown toad. With its bulging eyes and wide mouth.

"Are you volunteering to kiss the toad?" asked Innes.

"It may not be a toad prince. It may be a toad princess. Maybe you should kiss it."

Innes laughed. "Prince or princess, I don't mind. But you'd think if it wanted a kiss it would be friendlier."

Molly said, "Toad, if you want one of us to kiss you, just a quick kiss to break your curse, please hop or walk or crawl, or whatever toads do, right up to whoever would be most use to you."

The toad looked at Molly, then at Innes, then at Beth, then at Atacama. It leapt off the desk, legs splayed, and landed on the wooden floor.

Molly held her breath, hoping it wouldn't walk towards her.

The toad turned its lumpy back on all of them and waddled towards the door instead.

Innes shrugged. "If you'd rather stay a toad, we'll try not to be offended..."

Beth opened the door for the toad, then said, "Let's discuss plans for tomorrow over supper."

Molly picked up her bag and followed the others across the farmyard to another old barn. "Aren't we staying in the farmhouse?"

"Witches like their privacy," said Beth. "She converted this barn into a bunkhouse for her residential courses."

Innes shoved the door open, and Molly walked into a warm kitchen with a long wooden table heaped with plates, cutlery, scones, butter and a large jam jar. At the side of the room, wooden stairs led upwards, presumably to bedrooms.

Innes slumped on a chair and picked up a knife.

Atacama jumped onto the seat beside him. "The toad obviously doesn't feel part of the team, so let's split into pairs tomorrow." The sphinx turned his golden eyes towards Beth.

"Ok, ok. I'll take Molly." Beth looked at Molly. "I'll go with you to your neighbour, in case he tries to throw curses or dog dirt at you again. Then you come to my wood, while I interview… who do you think, Innes? Uncle Pete is the oldest, but Aunt Jean tells more family stories."

"Speak to both. The more information the better, I suppose." He stabbed the knife into the butter.

"Who will you speak to, Innes?" Beth asked.

He didn't answer.

Beth frowned. "Atacama, will you have to find your curse-caster?"

The sphinx shrugged. "I've no idea where he is. But I already know that he'll only lift my curse if I give him the answer to my riddle, which I will never do. I'll dig up the answers Mrs Sharpe wants, but I already know my curse must be broken, not lifted."

Molly said, "What's the difference between breaking and lifting?"

"Here we go. Curses for beginners again," muttered Beth.

Atacama smiled at Molly. "A curse is lifted if the conditions of the curse have been fulfilled or if the curse-caster relents and removes the curse. A curse is broken if you find a way round the curse or defeat the curse-caster. The first is what Mrs Sharpe teaches. The second is more difficult, more dangerous, and probably what I'll have to do."

"But everyone who comes here, every year, gets their curse lifted, don't they?" said Beth.

"That's what she advertises, so I'll be interested to see what she does at the end of the week if we haven't either found our curse-casters and apologised to their satisfaction, or fulfilled the conditions of the curse. Perhaps the witch is powerful enough to break our curses using her own magic."

Molly picked up a scone. "The flyer said 'Guaranteed result'. So perhaps we just have to try hard to lift the curses on our own, prove we deserve her help, then she'll do it for us at the end of the week."

The sphinx nodded.

Innes was digging the knife into the butter as if he was still digging up tatties.

"What's wrong, Innes?" asked Molly. "Are you worried about going with Atacama? You obviously know Beth's family, and they probably prefer kelpies to humans, so if you want to swap, I don't mind."

"It's not asking about Atacama's curse that's worrying me. It's asking about my own."

"But don't you just have to ask your dad?"

Innes put the butter knife down very carefully, as if he was concentrating on not doing something dangerous with it. "Yes. I have to ask my dad. And you know how you didn't want to tell us about your curse because you were embarrassed? All you'd done was get dog dirt on your leg. My dad got the entire family cursed and my big brother killed, and he's considerably more than embarrassed about that. If we even mention it he gets violently angry. He's ignored me for weeks, ever since I registered for this workshop.

"I hoped I could lift my dad's curse without discussing it with him. But now, to do Mrs Sharpe's homework properly, I'll have to force my father to tell me exactly what awful thing he did to get our family and rivers cursed. He won't want to tell me. And I'm not sure I can bear to listen."

Chapter Seven

Molly and Beth, who had shared a bedroom at the top of the stairs, got up before anyone else. Atacama was still snoring when they were ready to leave, though Innes was sitting blearily at the table with the toad, eating toast.

Molly had fallen asleep too fast to consider the most diplomatic way to interview Mr Crottel about the jobby-throwing incident, so she hoped to use the long walk to his house to come up with a plan. But when they left the bunkhouse, Beth strode towards a small shed with a faded sign on the door:

Bikes and broomsticks for use of students during residential courses only. Please clean your vehicle after use and fix any burst tyres or bent twigs.

Aggie Sharpe

Molly didn't spot any broomsticks as she pulled out a couple of helmets and a purple bike, but she couldn't see right to the back of the shed.

Beth chose a big green bike with a wicker basket, then cycled off fast along the farm track, well ahead of Molly.

At this speed, they'd be through Craigvenie and at Mr Crottel's house on the northern edge of town in ten minutes. Molly had to come up with a plan quickly.

"What do we say to him?" she yelled at Beth, as they passed the tall castellated clock tower in the town centre.

"How about 'sorry'?" Beth yelled back.

Molly sighed. She didn't think she should have to apologise for shouting at a man who had thrown dog dirt at her. Surely Mr Crottel should apologise for the filthy pavement and the potentially fatal curse. But he was the one with the magical powers, and she was the one with the dangerous habit of turning into a small edible mammal.

So, even though Molly didn't feel sorry, it probably would be wise to apologise anyway.

While they were pedalling down the main street of Craigvenie, Molly heard lots of people greet Beth by name. A man outside the bakers called, "Hello Beth, how's your Auntie Jean?"

They all clearly knew her, but did they know she was a dryad?

Then a mum pushing a baby in a buggy shouted, "Hey Beth, the woods are looking lovely this autumn! Well done!"

Molly glanced back. The woman was wearing a trendy jacket and carrying a gold handbag. She didn't look like someone who would believe in magic or spells or tree spirits. Maybe she just thought Beth liked the woods.

They reached Aunt Doreen's cottage at the end of the row of houses opposite the distillery, with its warehouses and pagoda roofs, and the cooperage yard, with its piles of barrels.

The upstairs lights were on in the end cottage, and the hens were making a cheerful noise at the back, but the front door wasn't open yet. Aunt Doreen was probably still in her dressing gown. Molly didn't want to disturb her, or find out whether her aunt had deliberately enrolled her on a workshop run by a witch, so she kept following Beth.

Beth pedalled past the splattery piles of brown on the pavement, stopped a few houses further on and hid her bike behind a low wall. Molly lifted her bike over too.

As they walked back towards his house, Molly asked, "What do you know about Mr Crottel?"

"Same as you: he's a witch, he's grumpy and he's lazy. He arrived here a few years ago, so no one knows who trained him. He doesn't visit my wood for herbs, so I've never spoken to him. As far as I know he's not a particularly powerful magic user, but he has a reputation for being snappy and vindictive."

"If he's not powerful, how did he change me into a hare?"

Beth shrugged. "Shapeshifting is complex magic, but everyone has a favourite spell, so perhaps that's his. And your change never lasts long, so perhaps he didn't have to put much power into the curse."

Molly said, "You know almost as much about spells and curses as Atacama. Do you know how to get Mr Crottel to lift my curse?"

"No. You'll have to work that out yourself."

Molly stepped carefully across the disgusting pavement outside Mr Crottel's garden and looked through an iron gate set in a high hedge.

"He isn't in the front garden. Maybe we should come back later..."

"Or you could knock on his door."

"I don't want to go into the garden. What if he throws more smelly things at me? What if his dogs are loose in the garden?"

Beth shrugged. "It's your curse. You might have to do unpleasant things to lift it. If you don't want to go in, we can head to the woods now and deal with my curse instead."

Molly put her fingers through the black curls of metal, unhooked the latch and pushed the gate open. It made exactly the rusty creaky eerie noise that Mrs Sharpe's red door didn't make.

Molly stepped into the garden, which was filled with soggy cardboard boxes of dog food tins, broken furniture, weeds and outdoor lights stuck at odd angles along the path. But at least there was no dog dirt.

"It's all on the pavement," muttered Molly.

She walked up the path towards the flaking green front door.

She knocked, gently and politely. There was no answer.

Then, just as she raised her hand to bang harder, the door opened slowly. Mr Crottel stood in the doorway, dressed in a stained greeny-grey three-piece suit, with a squint red-and-green-striped tie. "What do you want?"

"You might not remember, Mr Crottel, but I'm Molly Drummond, Doreen Drummond's great-niece, and earlier this week we had a bit of a… discussion about the… em… pavement, and we both shouted at each other, and I might have been a bit rude, then you waved your hands at me and… em… I wondered if you might have accidentally cursed me, so that I turn into a hare…?"

Mr Crottel stared at her, no expression on his grey stubbly face, as she stumbled through her badly prepared explanation. When she stopped talking, he smiled. "Ah, yes. You're the loud annoying child. No, I didn't accidentally curse you."

"Are you sure? Because since then, whenever I hear a dog bark or growl, I change…"

"How dare you doubt my word? I didn't *accidentally* curse you. The curse was entirely deliberate and I'm delighted to hear it's working. Do you regret being rude about my dogs yet?"

Molly sighed. "Yes, I completely regret everything I said about you, your dogs, your garden and anything brown that might have landed on my shoe. Now I'd like to apologise. I'm sorry. I really am very sorry. So…"

She paused, hopefully.

Mr Crottel raised his hairy eyebrows. "So what?"

"So could you please lift the curse?"

"Why?"

"Because it's done its job. I'm really sorry now."

"No. If I lifted my own curse, it would make me look weak and indecisive, then other dark-magic users would lose respect for me. Also, I hear that those who feed off curses are angered by curse-casters who lift their curses fast or frivolously. So, no, I'll leave the curse as it is."

"But..." Molly glanced round at Beth, who was standing on the path halfway between the doorstep and the closed gate.

Beth shrugged.

Molly turned back to Mr Crottel. "But I've said I'm sorry, and if you don't lift the curse I might get killed by a dog or eaten by a fox or run over or shot..."

"And wouldn't that be a perfect way to end your story?" He started to close the door.

She thought frantically. What other questions was she meant to ask? "Em... are there limits to the curse? Is there a quest or a task I can do to lift it?"

He shook his head. "No limits. The curse will stay with you until you die. And I won't accept any tasks either."

"Not even if..." Molly wrinkled her nose, "not even if I clean up the pavement?"

"Not my pavement, not my problem. Clean it up if you like, I'll make a mess of it again tomorrow."

Molly knew shouting wouldn't help, so with her fists

clenched to keep her voice calm, she said, "But that's not fair. Isn't there *anything* I can do?"

"Avoid dogs or run fast!" He grinned, showing his stained brown teeth. "I wonder how fast you can run?" He raised his voice. "Mash, come here and bark!"

Molly backed away, as a small black terrier trotted to Mr Crottel's ankle and stared at her. But the dog didn't make a sound.

Mr Crottel shouted, "Banger, come here. Bark for me."

Molly yelled, "Open the gate, Beth!"

But Mr Crottel jerked his fist and the gate made a grinding noise.

Beth called, "I can't, he's locked it!"

A tall grey wolfhound appeared at the door and stared at Molly silently.

"Come on, doggies, sing with me." Mr Crottel started to sing in a whiny voice: *"Run rabbit, run rabbit, run run run..."*

Both dogs joined in, whining, barking and howling.

And Molly shifted.

She was getting more used to this hare body and was recovering more quickly from the hot sensation in her bones, so she whirled round instantly and ran for the gate, where Beth was tugging unsuccessfully on the latch. Molly tried to find a hare-sized space to squeeze through, but the gaps in the gate's tightly wound spirals of metal were too small.

Mr Crottel stopped singing and shouted, "Chase the rude nasty child! Chase her!"

Suddenly Molly felt fangs digging into her fur and lifting her into the air.

She wriggled and jerked, desperate to escape.

Then she heard, "Calm down, I've got you."

They weren't fangs she could feel: they were Beth's fingers clutching her tight.

"I've got you," said Beth. "I'll keep you safe."

Molly relaxed. Then she saw the dogs tearing down the path towards them. Beth held Molly to her chest and the two dogs skidded to a halt at her feet.

Mr Crottel screeched, "Don't stop, boys. Catch her! Bite her!"

The small dog leapt at Beth's legs, the large dog leapt at Beth's face, and Beth fell back against the gate with a clatter.

Molly realised that if she stayed in Beth's arms, the dogs would attack them both.

So she jumped free, right over the head of the huge dog, and ran across the thin grass. She leapt over ripped chair cushions and bent cardboard boxes. The dogs turned their backs on Beth and chased Molly again.

She ran to the wall of the house, then turned in mid-leap and ran in the other direction. The dogs howled in frustration. She ran to the hedge, searching for a way through.

But the hedge was made of harsh boxy bushes, almost solid with intertwined branches and twigs. There were no gaps anywhere. And it was much higher than the wall she'd jumped yesterday.

Molly could see the small dog bouncing up and down, barking beside Mr Crottel's feet, and the big dog stalking towards her.

She ran along the side of the hedge, but the wall of leaves was tightly packed the whole way round the house. There was no escape.

And she was an obvious target, running in a straight line along the edge of the garden. Both dogs were chasing her again now.

"Look out!" yelled Beth.

Molly could see the danger. The two dogs were coming at her from different directions...

Mr Crottel laughed. "Run all you like, you won't get out of here."

"She'll shift back eventually," shouted Beth. "She never stays a hare for long."

"She won't shift back unless she crosses the boundary of my land, but I've left her no exit. She'll have to keep running until I call my dogs off. And I'm not sure I'll ever do that."

Molly ran away from the impenetrable hedge and straight at the terrier hurtling towards her. She leapt over the small dog and ran to the other side of the garden, dodging thorny roses and jumping over weed-filled flowerbeds.

She saw Beth crouching by the hedge near the gate and hoped the dryad hadn't been injured when the dogs leapt at her.

Molly ran in crazy loops and at acute angles round the messy garden, outpacing and evading the dogs again and again. But there were two of them and they were working together, and eventually one final foolish change of direction led her right into a corner.

She turned round. Both dogs, dripping drool and growling, were pushing their heads at her, snapping their teeth. Behind her, two unbroken lengths of hedge met at a right angle. Molly had nowhere to go. She was trapped.

Chapter Eight

Molly was cornered. There was no space between the two dogs, there was no space either side or behind her. They could enjoy ripping her apart in their own time.

Beth shouted, "Molly, over here!"

Molly saw a small hole opening up in the hedge. The bush beside Beth was twisting its branches apart to make a gap near the gate.

But it was too far away. There were two slavering dogs between Molly and this sudden, surprising exit.

Then she realised that two dogs might be easier to escape from than one dog.

Molly feinted to the left, so the big dog took a step that way. She feinted to the right, so the little dog skipped that way. Then she dived between them, leaping past their ears and ribs and tails. She heard them snarl in shock as they both turned at the same time to snap at her, and snapped at each other instead – because she had already landed and bounced and run away.

Molly sprinted towards the hedge, leaving the two dogs

fighting behind her. She leapt through the tunnel of skinny branches and hard leaves.

And Molly hit the pavement.

She was so relieved to be out of the garden and back in her human form, she didn't even mind that her elbow had landed in a soft pile of Banger or Mash's dog dirt.

She stood up and unzipped her filthy fleece.

Then she remembered Beth.

Beth was still stuck in the garden with two dogs, an angry witch, a locked gate and a hole in the hedge big enough for a hare, but not for a girl.

Molly ran to the gate.

Beth was standing with her hand on the latch, looking at the witch on his doorstep. Beth said calmly, "Mr Crottel, I'm impressed with the strength and wit of your curse on the human girl. But I know you don't want the trees or your own hedge turning against you. So please open your gate and I will ask your hedge to return to its shorn shape."

Mr Crottel bowed his head to Beth. Beth nodded back to him. The gate swung open.

As Beth left the garden, Mr Crottel shouted at Molly: "See, child. That's how to speak to a witch. With a bit of respect!"

Beth closed the gate, whispered to the hedge, then walked back to the bikes.

Molly rolled her fleece up with the stains on the inside. She glanced at the hedge, which was easing back into its previous shape.

She ran after Beth. "Did he let you go because you spoke to him politely? I was polite too, and he didn't let me go."

Beth picked up her bike and turned to look at Molly. A long considering look. Molly glanced down at her ripped jeans, her manky fleece, her scraped hands.

Beth shook her head. "You really don't fit into our world, do you?" Then she sighed. "The witch let me go because I carry the power of the trees within me and he's not strong enough to stand against me. I was always safe in his garden."

"I didn't realise that. I jumped out of your arms because I thought his dogs would hurt you."

Beth climbed onto her bike. "Really? I thought you just panicked."

"No, I was trying to..."

But Beth had ridden off.

Molly followed on her bike, trying to cycle like a girl going in a straight line, rather than a hare zigzagging all over the place.

Molly caught up with Beth at the clock tower, where the dryad took the road to the right.

"I didn't panic, you know," Molly gasped as she drew up close to Beth.

"You don't have to explain. Hares get frightened, I know that."

"But I'm not a hare. Even when I am a hare, I mean. I don't think like a hare, I just look like one."

"You move like a hare. And I felt you shiver in my arms."

Molly didn't want to think of herself as a shivering scared animal. "I didn't panic. It was a plan to draw the dogs away from you. Really."

Beth shrugged. "Whatever." She put on another burst of speed as they headed out of town.

Now Molly could see the wood they were cycling towards. Not the dark green straight lines of a forestry plantation, but the more colourful and varied outlines of a patch of old-growth woodland.

Beth leapt off her bike and propped it against the first tree she came to. She walked into the wood, then stopped to place her hand flat on the bark of a tall silver birch.

Molly followed her in, took a deep breath and said, "Thanks, Beth. Thanks for opening the hedge and—"

"Shhhh," said Beth, "don't interrupt."

Molly wondered if there was any point in talking to this girl at all. She watched as Beth laid her cheek against the tree like she was listening to it.

Molly was beginning to accept that magic existed. It was hard to deny when she regularly turned into a hare. But listening to trees? That seemed unlikely.

Though as she stood still, Molly could hear the tree too. Not words, but a gentle hiss and whisper in the air as the delicate leaves and supple twigs moved above in a tiny breeze. She glanced up and listened harder, wondering if there was meaning on the edge of the whisper.

"Come on, don't just stand about gawking," said Beth.

Molly looked down. Beth wasn't leaning against the tree any more, she was standing with her arms folded, frowning. She whirled round and marched off, and Molly followed her past more birch trees, as well as bright rowans and tall pines, and a few trees that Molly thought might be sycamores, geans and beech trees.

There was grass and clover underfoot, but also fallen leaves, as autumn reached slowly into the woods. There were a few red berries among the yellow leaves and pine cones on the ground, and sturdy mushrooms pushing up through the leaf litter.

But Molly couldn't stop to look, because Beth was striding ahead. Molly wondered whether she should follow or just wait with the bikes.

"What am I here for anyway?" she asked, her voice too loud in the soft rustling quiet of the wood. "Do you want me to take notes when we're speaking to your family? Should I ask questions if I think of any?"

"No, just sit still and be quiet."

"Maybe if you tell me about the curse before we get there, I'll be able to help."

"No human can help. It's a human curse that's killing this wood." Beth took a few steps to her right and pointed to a large bare circle of earth, dotted with windblown leaves, but with no plants growing on it. "Look!"

"Look at what? There's nothing there."

"Absolutely. Nothing growing, nothing alive. Look at the trees around it."

Molly looked up. The two pine trees nearest the bare earth had black scars on their trunks and were missing a few branches. It looked like both trees had been…

"Burnt. They're burnt! Is someone setting fire to your trees?"

Beth nodded, her lips pale and her eyes wet. "Someone who died more than three hundred years ago."

"A dying curse? Isn't that the strongest kind?"

"The cruellest kind, because we can't negotiate with the curse-caster and get it lifted."

"That doesn't always work even if they are alive," said Molly. "Mr Crottel isn't going to lift my curse."

"You didn't approach him right. You annoyed him even more."

"If you'd had a better idea, you should have suggested it beforehand!"

"I got you out of there…"

"And I've already tried to say thank you." Molly could feel herself losing patience with Beth, who seemed determined to take offence at everything Molly said or did. But she could also see how upset Beth was, standing beside the burnt trees, so she took a deep breath, and said, "Let's forget about my curse for a minute and think about yours. Who's burning your trees?"

"A witch. A human with nasty dark magic."

"A dead witch?"

"Dead, but still causing trouble. Her name was Meg Widdershins. Her real name was probably Meg Smith or something, but she was known as Meg Widdershins. She took advantage of local families by making their cows run dry and giving their children coughs and sneezes so she could demand money to heal them with herbs. When the families realised she was tricking them, she was burnt in the town square.

"As she died, she cursed the families who'd accused her, and she also cursed the trees whose branches were burning her. She cast a curse so that every year, in the month of her death, a member of each family died and a tree in this wood burned. Over the generations, those families lost so many members they no longer exist, but the wood still loses one tree every year."

Molly looked around. There must be thousands of trees in this wood. Surely losing one tree a year wasn't too bad? Not like a person dying. But she didn't say that out loud.

"Does someone sneak in and set fire to the tree? Couldn't you just catch and stop whoever it is?"

"You don't understand how it works. It's a *curse*, it happens by magic. The tree just starts to burn, with no match or spark or lightning setting it off. No warning either. We never know which tree it will be, or which day in October.

"The tree flares up like a torch, burns to a pillar of ash, then collapses to the ground. The dryad who cares for that tree burns too." Beth held out her arm, pulling up her black sleeve, and Molly saw a shiny jagged burn near her elbow.

"That was last year. The tree that stood here. A mature

birch with a black base because her older silver had worn away. She'd been here so long that three of us had cared for her, but she still had many strong years in her. Then she burnt in one flash of heat and pain and terror. And I burnt too.

"And this," she pulled down her top to show a red line on her shoulder, "this tree burnt nine years ago. She wasn't an old tree, she was slim and flexible. She burnt when I was only a tiny child and left this scar. It's my first real memory. Me screaming and my family running towards a screaming tree.

"We can't save the curse-hit tree once it starts to burn. The tree can be soaking wet, but that doesn't stop the fire. It's like the tree is burning from the inside. And when a birch burns, it feels like I'm burning from the inside too." Beth looked up at the charred trees above her. "All we can do is save the nearby trees, and we don't always manage that fast enough."

She stood in the middle of the bare patch. "No tree will ever flourish here again. Small plants might struggle through. But we can never get a tree to grow where the curse has burnt." Her voice shook as she said, "So, over time, the whole wood will burn and no trees will grow here at all."

Molly wanted to hug Beth, to offer sympathy, but she suspected the dryad would shove her away. So she said, "You know lots about the curse already. Perhaps you could fill in the homework sheet yourself?"

"I know about the effects of the curse on me and the trees. I don't know the whole history. Most of my family love old gossip, so we'll work through Mrs Sharpe's questions with them." Beth strode off again.

Molly looked round more closely and saw that the random lines of healthy trees were interrupted by frequent gaps where nothing grew. Losing one tree every year was enough, over a long time, to destroy this wood. Beth's wood was beautiful, but it was slowly dying.

Chapter Nine

Deep in the wood, surrounded by a perfect circle of trees, Molly saw a big house.

A big wooden house.

"A *wooden* house?" Molly blurted out. "But...? How...? Why...? I thought..."

Beth let Molly make a spluttering fool of herself for a few seconds, then said calmly, "We don't cut down trees, but when trees fall, we don't leave them all to rot either. A tree can have a new life in the things we create with its wood. So of course we live in a wooden house."

"And what do you do for... you know... cooking and lighting?"

"Ovens and lightbulbs, of course. This is the twenty-first century." Beth grinned at Molly's confusion. "But we light real fires sometimes too. I love woodsmoke and toasted cheese. But we only burn fallen wood, we don't rip trees apart to steal living wood."

Beth climbed the wooden steps to the varnished back door and pushed it open. "I'm home!"

A voice answered, "Has Aggie thrown you out? Were you rude about witches, or did you refuse to do your homework?" A round woman with cherry-red hair was laying cakes on cooling racks on the kitchen table, a little girl by her side. An old man was snoozing in a rocking chair.

"I'm here to *do* my homework, Jean." Beth turned to Molly. "This is my Aunt Jean, my Uncle Pete, and my teeny tiny pesky little cousin Rosalind. This is my classmate Molly. Mrs Sharpe wants us all to ask questions about our curses. Molly, did you bring the questions?"

Molly said hello and washed her grotty hands at the kitchen sink, then pulled out her own question sheet, which had nothing written on it because Mr Crottel hadn't given her any positive answers. "Didn't you bring a worksheet?"

"I don't like paper. It's not a sustainable use of wood. I prefer writing on a tablet."

Beth sat down and reached for the cakes on the nearest rack. Her Aunt Jean moved them to the other side of the table.

Molly sat down too. "Is that why you're getting Innes to take all the notes?"

"That and the fact he's trying to become the perfect pupil all of a sudden, in his desperation to be top of this class. If you write the answers while I ask the questions, I suppose that might be helpful."

As Molly hunted for a pen in her pocket, she felt a tap on her leg and looked down.

The little girl, who had red cheeks and dark hair pulled up into two bouncy bunches, was offering her a cake. "I baked this cake all myself. It's probably a horrid cake, because the one I ate was soggy in the middle and burnt on the outside. But I made it and it's a present, so you have to say thank you. If it really *is* horrid, then you can give it back once you've said thank you, and I won't be offended. Then I'll feed it to the birds, because they're not fussy. And next time you come I'll bake you a better cake. I'll bake it for longer in the middle so it's properly crumby and I'll bake it for less time on the outside so it isn't burnt."

The little girl handed Molly a plate with a sad saggy grey cake on it.

Molly smiled. "Thank you!" She nibbled the least burnt bit.

Rosalind stared at Molly. "It's horrid, isn't it?"

Molly nodded.

Rosalind giggled. "I knew it would be horrid! I'll feed it to the birds under my rowan trees." She took the plate and hopped out of the door.

Molly looked around the table. "Is Rosalind a dryad too? For rowan trees?"

Beth nodded. She'd managed to grab one of Jean's perfect golden cakes, so her mouth was full.

"If she's a dryad for rowans, why isn't she called Rowan? It's a real girl's name and it sounds lovely."

Beth swallowed. "Then we couldn't tell the difference between her and all the other rowan dryads who've

looked after this wood, or the rowan dryads working in other woods right now. It would be like naming a human child 'Girl' or 'Boy'. Everyone needs their own name. I am Beth of the Birches. She is Rosalind of the Rowans."

Molly nodded. "So, is your mum a silver birch dryad too?"

"We don't have parents." Beth sat up straighter and her voice grew sharper, with a mix of defensiveness and pride. "We don't need them. Each of us is found in a tree, the day after the previous dryad of those trees dies. At the foot of a tree, or in the branches, or in a hollow trunk. It's like a treasure hunt, searching for the new baby in the family.

"I found Rosalind, didn't I?" She grinned at the little girl, who was skipping back in with an empty plate. "I found her wrapped in a bright red blanket under a rowan tree, gazing at the leaves above her, and I gave her a hug..." Beth gave Rosalind another hug, as the little girl stretched up for an unburnt cake. "We call ourselves cousins and aunts and uncles. The trees of our kind are our brothers and sisters. That's why I won't let any more of them burn."

Jean pushed the rack of golden cakes towards Molly, who murmured thanks and took one. Then Jean said, "Shall I call the others to help with your questions, Beth?"

"No, you and Uncle Pete know more about this than anyone else in the house."

Beth looked at Molly's sheet. "The first question is: *Who cast the curse?*"

Uncle Pete opened his eyes, bright in his dark creased cheeks, and answered, "Meg Widdershins. You know that, Beth."

Molly asked, "What was her real name?"

Beth frowned. "Shhh."

"But you said it probably wasn't her real name. I just wondered if anyone knows her real name."

Uncle Pete answered, "It was Wilkie. Margaret Wilkie."

Molly wrote down:

Meg Widdershins,

real name: Margaret Wilkie.

Then she asked, "Was that her married name or her, what do you call it, maiden name?"

Uncle Pete said, "I've no idea. But I know it was the name on the legal documents. 'Margaret Wilkie, also known as Meg Widdershins'. Same initials, that's why I remember it from when my uncles and aunts told me the story."

Beth sighed. "Molly, if you insist on writing down two answers for every question, this is going to take ages..."

Aunt Jean said, "Your friend has the right idea, Beth. If you want to do your homework thoroughly, you should do more than you were asked to do."

Beth snapped, "I didn't say she was my friend, I said she was my classmate. Second question: *When was the curse cast?*"

Jean and Pete spoke in unison: "Dawn on seventeeth of October 1661."

"What time is dawn?" asked Molly, her pen poised over the paper.

This time Jean sighed. "Don't you know when the sun rises each day, child?"

Molly shook her head.

Beth said, "It's just before 8 a.m. in mid-October. But it doesn't really matter, because the curse lasts all month, and the tree might burn any day, any time in October."

"It does matter, Beth, because it's another answer on the sheet. Remember, this is all about impressing Mrs Sharpe with teamwork and attitude and effort, and I didn't get any answers from Mr Crottel, apart from a big fat smelly 'NO', so let's gather lots of long answers here."

Pete murmured, "Mr Crottel? He's a nasty one. Never says thank you to any plant or tree. If he cursed you, he won't lift it out of kindness or remorse. I hope our answers will help Aggie find another way. What's the next question?"

"*Why was the curse cast?*" said Molly and Beth together.

"Because the local people, in their rush to burn Meg Widdershins as a witch, didn't bother to find dry dead firewood," explained Jean. "Or possibly they wanted the fire to burn slow and painful. So they chopped down trees from this wood, sliced logs and kindling from the fresh damp timber, and burnt Meg Widdershins with greenwood smoke and flames. It was a cruel thing to do, both to the woman and to the trees. But she didn't notice the trees' pain, she only felt her own. She cursed those who burnt her and the wood they used.

"It was a dying curse, conjured from agony and terror. I should feel sorry for her, but I've lost so many of my trees and my loved ones' trees, that I can't find any spare pity for her."

Molly looked at the next question. "I think you've just answered this, but—"

Beth read out loud: "*Was the curse justified and reasonable, or disproportionate?*"

Aunt Jean and Uncle Pete looked at each other.

In the brief silence, Molly realised Rosalind was sitting under the table, murmuring a rhyme about berries and playing with Molly's laces.

Then Uncle Pete said, "Meg Widdershins wasn't in a situation where reason was easy for her to grasp. She was dying, so it probably seemed entirely justified, reasonable and proportionate to her. But she's killed hundreds of people, weakening a dozen local families so effectively that now no humans die by her curse, because none of the original accusers' descendants are left. And she's still destroying trees and causing grief and pain to dryads who never hurt her at all. So, no, it was not justified, reasonable or proportionate."

Rosalind stopped chanting verses over Molly's toes

and said clearly, "People do silly things when they're scared."

Aunt Jean ducked her head under the table. "Yes, they do darling. But *you* don't need to be scared. Beth will save our trees by asking these questions."

Rosalind started murmuring again, "One berry, two berries, three berries RED! Four berries..."

Beth asked, "*Was it a dying curse?*"

Molly wrote Yes, before everyone else said it, then Beth read out, "*Are there limits to the curse?*"

Jean answered, "Yes. The limits were when the families died out, which happened in the nineteenth century, and when the wood no longer exists. It's a slow death, much slower than hers."

"Was the curse written down? Do you know the exact words?" asked Molly.

Jean nodded. "It's written in our hearts and the words burn again each autumn."

They all said it, even Rosalind under the table:

"For this agony, I curse every man and woman round this fire. Each of your families will lose one member to a burning death by fever each October, until none of your blood live on this land. And I curse the woodland that tortures me with unbearable smoke and heat. One tree will burn each October, until that wood is bare dead earth. This is the promise I make with my death."

There was silence in the kitchen, until Rosalind started murmuring again. "One berry, two berries, three berries

RED!" She shifted so she was leaning warmly against Molly's leg. "Four berries, five berries, the trees are all..."

Molly started to write the curse down, but she couldn't remember it all. Beth took the pen. "Let me."

Molly read the next question. "*Does the curse specify a task or quest that will lift the curse?*"

Pete shook his head.

So Beth read, "*Is the curse-setter still living?*"

No wrote Molly.

"Are any of her family still living?" Molly asked, hoping to fill in more space on the sheet. "Did she have children? Are there any Wilkies still around here?"

Pete said, "No, there are no local Wilkies descended directly from the witch because she had no sons, though there are couple of descendants through a daughter's line. But they haven't dabbled in magic for a long time."

Rosalind crawled out from under the table, right over Molly's feet, her knees crushing Molly's toes. She said cheerfully, "Auntie Jean! I know how to bake cakes that aren't horrid! I could put them out in the sunshine, that wouldn't burn them!"

Jean smiled. "Shush just now. Beth's doing her homework."

Beth read out: "*Would an apology help?*"

"Who could we apologise to? What would we apologise for?"

"*What would you sacrifice to be free of this curse?*"

"Isn't that a question for you, Beth?" Jean said softly.

Molly glanced at Beth, who was staring out the window at the trees around the house.

Molly opened her mouth to ask Jean something, and shut it again, afraid she'd offend her. Then she decided that offending dryads wasn't as bad as burning their trees, so she said, "Why is Beth doing this workshop? If Mrs Sharpe lifts the curses of everyone who goes on the workshop, why hasn't one of you done it before?"

"Aggie sets an age limit on this workshop, between eleven and twenty-one years old. Young enough to learn, she says. I suspect she's looking for folk fit enough to howk her tatties. But when she started these courses a few years ago, the rest of us were already too old, and Beth only turned eleven this summer. That's why Beth is doing it for all of us."

"There is another hard question," whispered Beth. "*Do you deserve to be free of this curse?*"

Jean and Pete looked at each other again. Beth rubbed her scarred arm.

Molly felt Rosalind, back under the table, tickling her ankle with the ends of the laces.

"Of course you deserve to be free of the curse." Molly wrote YES in big clear letters. "You didn't hurt this witch, your trees didn't do her any deliberate harm, you shouldn't still be suffering for what ignorant people did hundreds of years ago. Yes, you all deserve to be free of this curse."

"But do we deserve it more than our uncles, aunts and

cousins who suffered it over the years, when no one was offering a way out?" asked Jean quietly.

"Rosalind shouldn't have to suffer like you have," said Molly.

Beth took the pen from Molly's hand and wrote:

We deserve to be free of it.

"Any other questions?" asked Pete.

Molly had lots of questions. How could human-looking babies be born from trees? How did they communicate with their trees? Did all trees have a dryad? Were there dryads in every wood?

But Beth said, "No more questions. We've done our homework, we'd better get back to the tattie-lifting. It's hard work though," she said with a small smile, "and we haven't eaten since breakfast. Could we take a few cakes, please, Aunt Jean?"

"Of course. You could take all Rosalind's cakes..."

Rosalind giggled under the table. "Innes would eat my cakes. He eats anything, especially when he's a big squishy monster."

Jean laughed too. "You can take a bag of my cakes, so long as you share them with everyone on the workshop."

"Even the toad?" asked Molly. "We're not really sure what the toad eats."

"There's a cursed toad?" said Pete. "Oh yes, I think being nice to the toad is a very good idea."

They packed warm golden cakes into a paper bag, said goodbye to Jean and Pete, and hugged Rosalind. Then Molly and Beth walked back through the wood.

As they circled round three rowans with a pile of soggy grey cakes at their roots, Molly saw a robin peck up a crumb, tip its head to the side like it was considering the taste, then waggle its beak to shake the sticky crumb off. She smiled, then asked, "Was that useful, Beth? Did you find out anything you didn't know?"

"Not really, and I'd have found it out a lot faster if you hadn't insisted on showing off your ignorance by asking all those extra questions. I told Innes we shouldn't let a beginner, a *human*, onto the workshop. I knew you'd slow us down."

"What do you have against humans? I thought you went to the local school with human pupils?"

"Yes, but that's me in their world. That's safe. I don't do any harm there. I don't trust humans in my world."

"Why? Because of one human witch, one curse, three hundred years ago? You can't blame all humans for that!"

"It's not just the curse. And it's not all humans. Some people do respect trees, but most of you don't. There are humans damaging the trees' world all the time. Look!" Beth marched over to a gnarled old silver birch, with hearts, lightning bolts and initials carved into its wide trunk. "See! Humans and their blades cutting our trees. Attacking and assaulting and hurting and scarring!" Beth's voice cracked as she stroked the bark.

Molly sighed. She had never carved her initials into a tree, but she'd never thought it was a crime before either.

Then Beth gasped. "This one is still fresh." She shoved the bag of cakes at Molly, laid her hands either side of a botched splintery K hacked into the bark and murmured gentle words.

Molly waited quietly, not wanting to interrupt another dryad-to-tree conversation, nor to defend the vandal who had hurt this living tree.

When Beth patted the birch and stepped away, Molly saw that the trunk was still marked with a squint 'K', but it looked less wounded now, as if it had been scraped rather than hacked.

"Did you just heal the tree?"

"I encouraged her to knit the damaged cells back together. That's my job, to look after the trees. It's *not* my job to look after annoying humans in my wood, or in this magical world." Beth grabbed the cakes and strode off towards the bikes.

As Molly clambered onto her bike, she said, "Back to the farm and the tattie field?"

"So long as we dig at opposite corners."

Molly nodded. That was probably the best idea.

Chapter Ten

When Molly and Beth arrived back at the tattie field, they found three forks, a stack of empty red buckets and a lunch basket, but no one digging. Beth dropped the bag of the cakes onto the basket, picked up a fork and a bucket, then strode off to the far corner of the field.

Molly picked up a fork and pushed it into the claggy earth. "I'll meet you in the middle," she called.

Beth didn't answer.

Digging allowed Molly plenty of time to think, especially as she was pulling up fewer tatties than the day before, even though she was putting in as much effort. Working beside Innes, Atacama and the toad yesterday had gone much faster and more easily.

She knew she should be coming up with ways to change Mr Crottel's mind about lifting her curse. But it was hard to think about her curse without also remembering how terrified she'd been when the witch's dogs trapped her in the garden.

She found herself thinking about Beth instead. About

the unfairness of the curse on Beth's family, but also the unfairness of Beth blaming Molly for all the awful things humans had done to her trees.

She looked at Beth on the far side of the field, head down, digging and pulling. She found the dryad prickly, but fascinating. She'd love to know more about how dryads worked with the trees. But if Beth couldn't be friends with a human, there was no point pushing. Once they'd finished the course, they'd probably never see each other again.

She kept digging and loosening and howking. Molly found herself chanting as she worked. "Dig, wiggle, pull! Dig, wiggle, pull!" Soon she was waggling her shoulders and hips as she chanted. "Dig, wiggle, pull!" She smiled as she danced her tattie-howking dance.

She raised the fork in the air, chanting, "Dig, wiggle, pull! Dig, wiggle, pull..." and brought the four metal prongs down, right towards the big round eyes of the toad.

Molly gasped and jerked the fork away.

The toad didn't move. It just stared up at her.

She dropped the fork and crouched down. "I nearly speared you right through, you silly thing! Why did you creep up on me?"

The toad stared at her.

"I suppose you couldn't warn me, could you? Can toads even make a noise?"

The toad inflated its pale throat and made a sudden loud sound, like a fast drumming or hammering.

"So you *can* croak! Next time, please croak when you're getting close, so I don't aim a fork at you."

The toad croaked again.

"Was that a yes?"

The toad croaked again.

Molly smiled. "Now we're chatting, can you tell me if you found answers to your curse questions this morning?"

The toad croaked.

Molly frowned. "Is that a yes or just a croak? What about silence for no and croaking for yes?"

The toad croaked.

"Brilliant. So, did you find out more about your curse?"

The toad stayed silent.

"Can't you ask the person who cursed you?"

The toad just stared at her.

"Would that be too dangerous?"

The toad gave one small quiet croak.

"I'm sorry." Molly sighed. "So, do you know how to lift your curse?"

The toad didn't croak.

"Me neither." Molly smiled sympathetically at the toad. "But Mrs Sharpe will do it for us, won't she?"

The toad was silent.

Molly sighed. "I wonder if you understand any of what I'm saying..."

The toad croaked.

"Oh. Good. So, can I help you write your homework or anything?"

The toad was silent.

Molly stood up. "I'm happy to help, if you want. In the meantime, let's dig these tatties. I find singing as you work helps it go faster. You can sing the bass line..."

The toad croaked.

So the toad dug at one tattie shaw while Molly did a whole row, singing, "Dig, wiggle, pull! Dig, wiggle, pull! Dig, wiggle—"

Then a voice said loudly in her ear, "Are you dancing with the fork or the toad?"

She looked round at Innes, pale and hunched with his hands in his pockets, and Atacama, dark and calm with his tail flicking in the cool autumn air.

Molly laughed, "I think we're all dancing with the tatties. It's a bit boring otherwise! Now you're here, though, we can discuss what we found out today, which should make the digging go faster."

But Innes picked up a fork and walked to another corner of the field, muttering, "Even your singing would be better than talking about how my dad entirely deserves the curse that's killing his sons and his rivers."

Molly, Atacama and the toad watched him slouch away, but Beth yelled, "Oh no you don't, Innes! No one's going off in a huff today!"

Molly thought that was a bit of a cheek, after Beth had walked away from her so many times in the woods.

But she smiled as Beth chivvied everyone into Innes's corner, organised them digging neighbouring rows and

said, "We have to do as much homework as we can now, so Mrs Sharpe can teach us new stuff tonight. Let's share what we found out."

They dug, much faster than before, while Beth ran through the answers her Aunt Jean and Uncle Pete had given.

And Molly described her unpleasant encounter with Mr Crottel. "Even though he wasn't very cooperative, I did find out that he meant to curse me and that he won't lift it, and also I know that crossing boundaries is what shifts me back. So my homework was a bit scary, but it wasn't a waste of time."

Then she added, "I've chatted to the toad, and the toad hasn't spoken to the person who cursed him or her, and doesn't know of a way to lift the curse. Is that accurate?"

The toad croaked.

Molly said, "Yes, that's accurate."

She looked up, to see the rest of them staring at her.

Beth said, "You chatted to the toad?"

Molly nodded.

Innes muttered, "This human sings to tatties, dances with forks and chats to toads. It's a shame none of those are vital skills for lifting curses." He lunged forward and thrust his fork into the earth like he was eviscerating enemies.

Beth said, "It was you who thought involving her would be a good idea."

Atacama said, "It was a good idea. And working together was a good idea too, Innes, even if you're struggling to remember why just now."

Innes didn't answer, just threw a large potato so hard that the bucket tipped over.

Beth said, "We're stuck with each other just now, so let's make the best of it. What did you two find out?"

Innes said, "Why do we have to talk about it? Are we learning anything from each other's horror stories of death, destruction and dog jobby? Our task was to find these answers, not to discuss them all day like a group therapy session." His voice was cracking. "I don't see why you have to know all my family's business..."

Molly said quickly, "That's fine. We'll hear it when you tell Mrs Sharpe tonight, if you don't want to say it more than once."

He looked at her and nodded.

Beth said, "So, Atacama, did you find your curse-caster?"

Atacama shook his head and groomed his left ear.

"For goodness sake, cat. Can't you bear to tell us either?" snapped Beth. "We've told you everything."

Atacama said, "There's very little to tell. I don't know who cursed me, and there weren't any witnesses, so I couldn't interview anyone. But I returned to the site I was guarding when it happened..." His voice trailed away into a growl.

"Where is that?" asked Molly.

"It's beside a pyramid, obviously," said Innes.

"Really? A pyramid? In Speyside?"

Atacama said, "Yes. Until last week, I guarded a hidden entrance to our client's domain, in the back wall of the cooperage yard at the distillery, where the whisky barrels

are made and mended. There are lots of old casks stacked in wooden pyramids. It's a perfect place to hide a magical door and the sphinxes who guard it."

Molly had seen the high piles of rounded barrels every time she came to stay with her aunt, but she'd never thought of them as Scottish pyramids. "Who's your client and what's through the door in the wall?"

"I don't know. I'm a guard. I stop people entering or allow them past; I don't know where they go or whom they visit.

"So, Innes and I went to the pyramids, where we greeted my sister Caracorum, who is guarding the door today. Then Innes asked the questions on the sheet and pushed me to remember everything I could about the day I was cursed."

"And you showed me how you stopped your attacker getting through the door," interrupted Innes, sounding more enthusiastic than he had all day. "You must have had an amazing duel."

Innes turned to Beth, Molly and the toad. "Scars on the ground, claw marks on the casks. It was pretty impressive. Atacama fought him off single-handed! Single-pawed, anyway."

"I didn't win, though, did I?" murmured Atacama. "I'm cursed now, I'm no use to anyone."

"You stopped him getting in, so you did your job," Innes said firmly. "You've nothing to be ashamed of. Unlike... unlike some other people who've been cursed."

"If you fought with the curse-caster, why don't you know who it is?" asked Molly.

"I'll tell you the story I told Innes in the cooperage yard. One evening, when I was on duty, a pillar of whirling golden sand approached the pyramids. I stood up to block the door in the wall, and a voice demanded to be let past."

"What kind of voice?" asked Beth.

"I asked that too," said Innes. He pulled out a neatly folded piece of paper. "I wrote down: Adult male or perhaps putting on a deep voice; human or similar; English or maybe using a false accent. So, male or pretending to be, adult or pretending to be, human or pretending to be, and English or pretending to be. It could have been anything in that pillar of sand. Even our friend the toad here."

The toad backed off awkwardly and croaked.

Atacama said, "When the voice demanded to be let past, I refused politely but firmly, then asked my riddle. The voice said, 'I do not know the answer, but let me past anyway.'

"I said, 'Answer or leave.'

"He replied, 'If you do not let me past, then I will curse you, I will remove the very thing that makes you a sphinx. That is my answer, now let me past.'

"Of course I refused. So he cursed me. There was a blizzard of sand, which blinded me for a moment. When I could see again, he was still there. He hadn't got past me, but my mind was lighter by the words of one riddle.

"He said, 'Ask your riddle again, pussy cat, and I might answer this time.'

"But I couldn't ask. Because I had lost my riddle.

"He offered to lift the curse if I let him past. I refused. I pounced and bit and scratched through the swirling sand, but whatever was hidden inside just laughed and whirled away, saying as he left that I'd get my riddle back if I let him through the door.

"That's why I can't guard the entrance now. I have no riddle to ask. Also I'm a security risk because my family know I could get my riddle back by telling him the answer. But of course I never will, because even though I'm nothing without a riddle, I'm also nothing without my family's respect."

"Do you remember the answer?" asked Beth.

"Yes. I have the answer, but not the question. That's what's so frustrating. But I won't give that creature what he wants. I know how to lift my curse, because the curse-caster told me that when I was prepared to let him in I should scratch a message on a cask at the top of the pyramid opposite the door. But I'd rather be cursed forever than betray my vows."

Molly said, "Do you believe Mrs Sharpe can lift the curse without letting your curse-caster in?"

Atacama stared at the earth clogging his elegant paws. "I would hardly be digging up vegetables for her if I didn't believe it."

Chapter Eleven

The witch's packed lunch and the dryads' cakes gave them enough energy to get back to the tatties with more speed and less dancing.

"So, are there any similarities in our three curse stories?" asked Beth. "Any lessons we can learn?"

"Don't annoy people who can use magic," said Molly, knocking a clump of earth off her fork.

"Don't be flippant."

"No, really. That's the only common link. Me, Atacama, the people of Craigvenie, your trees, presumably the toad and Innes's dad too, we all annoyed someone who can cast spells. Whether we did something good or evil or just daft, we all annoyed someone with the power to take revenge. That's it. That's all we can learn. Don't annoy people who can use magic." She shrugged and started on the last row of tatties.

"But can we learn anything from the answers we gathered about how to lift the curses?" Beth asked.

"Only that lifting a curse often involves doing

something worse than the curse," replied Molly. "Doing something wrong, like Atacama is refusing to do. Or dying, because some curses don't end until the victim dies. There doesn't seem to be an obvious 'happy ever after' way of lifting any curse."

They were all quiet as they finished the last row.

Innes looked up at the sun. "Mrs Sharpe won't shut the shop for a while. I need to sit by running water. Does anyone want to join me? If you're all there, I'm less likely to dive in, swim off and never come back."

They walked across a field, through a narrow wood and over a path to a shallow burn running fast around moss-covered rocks.

"I thought kelpies were great big monsters under the water," said Molly. "But you must be able to shift into something small if you could swim away in that."

"We have deep river pools where we can stretch out in our largest shape. But in shallow water I can shift into a pike."

As they sat quietly, watching the water race past, Molly felt completely calm for the first time in days. She circled her shoulders, letting them relax after hours of digging.

To her left, Innes sat on a rock a few paces away from the rest of them. He'd pulled off his shoes and was dangling his feet in the water. His eyes were closed as if he was trying to relax, but his forehead was creased in a frown.

Atacama was sitting in his perfect pose, tail wrapped round his paws, ears pricked, like a carving of the ideal cat, but with a smooth dark human face and small sleek wings. He was staring at the water, as if he was thinking deep philosophical thoughts. Suddenly his paw flicked out and scooped a yellow leaf from the burn, tossed it into the air and batted it, like a kitten playing with a cat toy.

Molly laughed.

Atacama turned to her. "Reflexes," he said sternly. "I'm working on my reflexes."

She looked to her right. The toad was squatting by the edge of the burn, letting misty spray dampen its skin.

Molly asked, "Do you live by a river?"

The toad was silent.

"A pond, perhaps?"

Still silence.

"Do you live by water at all?"

More silence.

She sighed. Unless she was asking questions with 'yes' answers, she couldn't be sure she was having a conversation with the toad at all.

Beth said, "Hey, toad. Is this girl bothering you?"

The toad didn't answer that either.

Molly looked up at Beth. She was on a branch overhanging the water, filing her silver nails.

Molly knew that these people weren't her friends, that they didn't really care about her, that they were all caught up in their own problems. But at least all five of them were honestly and equally focussed on the same goal. Lifting their curses.

Then Beth whispered, "Humans coming! I think it's the Strachan family, they're usually fine. Atacama should hide in the shadows though, in case he gives them a fright."

Atacama stepped calmly behind Innes's rock and the toad crawled under a leaf.

Innes said, "But what about Molly? Don't the Strachans have a—?"

He was too late. Molly heard a high-pitched bark and as she stood to run away, she felt the heat in her bones and found herself rearing up on strong hind legs.

"Hide!" said Innes.

Molly looked round. She didn't want to hide behind the rock with the fanged meat-eating sphinx. So she just lay down, her tall ears along her back and her bright eyes closed.

"Ok. Don't hide," said Innes. "Lying down in clear view right beside the path might work too."

But Molly felt fine. Flat on the ground, with her soft brown fur and her smooth lines, she felt safe. She knew she was less visible staying still than running away.

She heard voices. Children chattering, adults rumbling and that high-pitched bark again. But she didn't look up. She didn't move at all.

She heard a woman's voice. "Hello Beth, and Innes, is it? Enjoying your holidays?"

Beth said, "Hello Mrs Strachan. Yes, thanks."

"Ok. We'll leave you in peace with your trees, and your fish, and… everything. Come on, kids."

Molly heard snuffling and scraping, and another bark. The dog was really close.

She kept her head down, hoping the shivers she could feel up and down her spine weren't showing in rippling fur…

She heard footsteps pass her as the family moved along the path. But the dog was still sniffing around.

"Shoo! Off you go," muttered Beth.

Molly heard a child's voice as the family walked away. "Is she the magic one?"

"Everyone is magic in their own way, Jocelyn. Let's go and play Poohsticks."

"But is her *hair* magic? Could I have magic hair?"

"I'll put magic sparkly bobbles in your hair when we get home. Come on…"

Then the dog barked. Right above Molly.

It was too close. It was going to step on her.

She opened her eyes and saw both Beth and Innes jump down to grab the dog. But Molly had already lost control. She couldn't stay still any longer. She leapt up and ran, in the opposite direction from the family, hoping the dog would follow them rather than her.

She heard Beth shout, "Ow! It bit me!"

And she heard the dog yapping behind her.

It was chasing her. But there was nowhere to leap or dodge. Just the open path, the water on one side, or the rocky ground on the other.

Molly had to run straight ahead. With a dog right behind her.

The dog barked again, high-pitched and close.

Molly realised the dog's bark was higher than the little girl's voice, and that the dog behind her was even smaller than she was. A tiny, hairy, ribboned Yorkshire terrier, sprinting towards her.

Molly whirled round and crouched down, facing the dog.

As the dog reached her, she reared up on her hind legs and punched the dog on the nose. Whack, whack, whack; left, right, left. Whacking down with both front paws, from *above* the dog.

The dog whined, turned tail, and ran away.

Molly loped back along the path, her long back legs clumsy under her. Going at any pace slower than a run felt awkward, because her hare body was designed to sprint, not saunter.

Innes, sitting on his rock, was laughing.

Beth was wrapping a leaf round her finger. She waved her hand at Molly. "That little rat bit me! While I was trying to save you *again*!"

Innes said, "You didn't need to save Molly; she can fight dogs off herself. Don't try that move with a Rottweiler though, Molly!"

Beth muttered, "I suppose it's only a scratch." She secured the leaf with a twist and sat down. "We could head for a boundary to change you back. Unless you're happy as a hare for now?"

Molly approached Beth and crouched at her feet.

Innes sighed. "Look at her. She's completely human, she was utterly ignorant of magic until this week, but she's still coping with her curse better than I am. I should stop being such a drama queen and just tell you what I've found out, shouldn't I?"

Beth said, "It's not long until this evening's class. Don't do it twice if you don't want to."

Innes shrugged. "I don't want to, but I think I should. We're meant to be a team."

Atacama and the toad reappeared and sat by Innes's rock.

Innes said, "I knew we'd been cursed because my father ate someone he shouldn't have eaten. But I didn't know who or why or what the conditions of the curse were. I know what the effects are though.

"I know that once a month, when the moon is visible in the sky, one of the tributaries to the Spey, one of our burns or rivers, turns from fresh water to salt, suddenly, without warning. Not diluted salt like sea water, but a thick, poisonous level of salt, which kills all life in the water.

"The first month the salt curse hit, my big brother Firth was caught in the water in his fish self. When we found him, he was caked in salt crystals, solid and heavy and crackling white. He was dead, and so were thousands of other water creatures."

Innes dipped his toes in the water again.

"When the moon leaves the sky, the salt vanishes. The water is fresh enough to drink again. But nothing is left

alive. And because a different burn or river is poisoned each month, eventually this whole water system, the whole Spey valley, will be dead. So will my family, because the curse is designed to kill us, one by one.

"I knew the curse had killed my brother and I knew Mum thought it was Dad's fault, because I've heard them arguing. They've always refused to tell me the details though, even when I signed up for Mrs Sharpe's workshop. But when I went home to the mill-house today, with Atacama at my back and with an official-looking bit of paper, Dad had to tell me."

"He was relieved to tell you," said Atacama.

"Do you think so?"

"Yes."

"So, tell us," said Beth.

Innes pulled the sheets of paper out of his pocket. He shook one open. "That's yours, Atacama. Your mysterious voice in the pillar." He laid that sheet on the rock and anchored it with a stone.

He smoothed out the other sheet. "This is the story of my dad's curse." He stared at it, frowning, rereading the answers under his breath. No one interrupted.

He shook his head. "The curse is entirely justified and completely deserved. But the curse is *not* reasonable or proportionate. Because it's not just punishing Dad, it's punishing all of us. Everyone and everything in the water. Is that reasonable or proportionate? Is it?"

Beth said gently, "We don't know, Innes, because you

haven't told us the answer to the most vital question. Why did someone curse him?"

Innes took a deep breath. "Late last year, my dad was swimming in the Spey, early in the morning, in his largest hungriest most monstrous self. He was so hungry he was considering turning into a horse and luring a human to eat, even though we have a family rule about not eating people close to home. Then he heard a noise above him."

They all looked up, even Molly. But Innes pointed to the water in front of them. "Not in the sky. He was underwater. He heard noises on the surface. Small ripples, little singing voices. He rose up and..."

Innes cleared his throat. "I wrote it down:

"He heard voices singing Happy Birthday and giggling.

"He saw a bark boat filled with fairies, wearing party hats made of heather blossom and waving balloons made of poppy petals.

"And this is what he did.

"He rose up out of the river, he opened his mouth and he ate them."

Innes folded the paper and put it under the stone.

"It was stupid. He didn't even like the taste, apparently. Too sweet. And it didn't satisfy his hunger. He had to hunt eels later in his pike self. But he ate them. Half a dozen fairy children at a birthday party.

"It was stupid. It was cruel. And it was wrong. We have

rules about what we hunt: we're not allowed to eat magical beings or human beings within the catchment area of our own river.

"So that's why we're cursed. I didn't know he'd done something so daft and so horrible. If he wasn't my dad, and if the curse hadn't killed my brother, I might think: fair enough, you deserve your curse, learn to live with it."

He sighed. "But I have to lift it. Or I will die, and my wee brother will die, and the rivers will die..." He gazed at the water.

Molly was frustrated that she couldn't ask questions. She sat up and flicked her ears.

"Was that a question?" asked Beth. "Perhaps we should work out a code..."

"I haven't said who the curse-caster is yet, that's probably what she wants to know. It was the fairy who organised the birthday party and who lost two of her own children and four of their best friends. The heather fairy." Innes picked up the paper again. "The limits are: The curse will last until my father has lost all his children to the salt or until the Spey and its tributaries are empty of life.

"I don't think Dad knew what to do when she cast the curse. He didn't tell anyone about it. The rest of the family only found out when my big brother died. I'm the next oldest, and the right age for this workshop, so I have to lift the curse."

"But no other kelpies have died since Firth, have they?" asked Beth.

"We try to keep out of the water on moonlit nights, but we can't remove every fish and frog and larva from every run of water. There's nowhere safe to put them, because we don't know where the curse will hit next. And it won't end until my father has lost me and my brother, or his river.

"Dad tried apologising to the fairy, but like Molly found out, not all curse-casters will accept an apology. So there's no point in me trying. Mrs Sharpe is my only hope.

"And this is all my dad's fault. Because he killed some fairies."

"But you can lift the curse," said Beth. "You just have to dig endless fields of tatties and keep doing your homework." She glanced at the fading sunlight on the tree trunks. "Time to head back."

Atacama said, "There may be more dogs on the path. Does someone wearing clothes want to hide Molly under their coat?"

Beth and Innes stared at each other.

Beth said, "Not really, to be honest."

Innes said, "She won't want to trust herself to a predatory kelpie. If we snack on fairies, hares might be on the menu too."

Beth sighed. "Alright then."

She scooped Molly up and they walked along the path, Molly perched uncomfortably in Beth's unwilling arms. Beth turned left and crossed the rough ground of the woods.

Suddenly Molly felt larger, heavier, more awkward.

Beth yelled and dropped her. Molly fell onto a hard heap of grey stones, bashing her knees.

"But that's not a boundary!" said Beth. "Mrs Sharpe's land doesn't start until the fence."

Innes pointed at the pile of stones, then swung his arm out to indicate several other piles in a line through the trees. "This must be an old wall. The magic must still regard this as the Skene Mains boundary."

Molly stood up. "Sorry. Thanks for carrying me."

"Thanks for dislocating my shoulder..." muttered Beth, as she clambered round the tumbledown wall and headed for the more modern fence.

Molly turned to Innes. "Is she that unfriendly to all humans, or just to me?"

"She has enough trees to make her happy, she doesn't need human friends. Don't take it personally. Let's give our answers to the witch and see what she wants us to do next, to earn our curse-lifting." He frowned and kicked at a stone. "I can't help thinking, if my dad had eaten a boatload of human children, their parents wouldn't have been able to curse him."

Molly asked, "So do you wish he had eaten a human birthday party instead of a fairy birthday party?"

Innes bit his lip. "Yes. I do. But most of all, I wish he hadn't eaten any birthday parties at all."

Chapter Twelve

When they got to the classroom, Molly opened the cupboard marked:

CURSE-LIFTING WORKSHOP SUPPLIES

She searched the shelves for more questionnaires.

The bottom shelf was filled with a heap of shiny chains, the next shelf up was covered in jam jars of pens and pencils, which Molly raided for a fresh pen, and the shelf at her eye-level was stacked with rolled-up parchment scrolls. But on the top shelf, she saw a whole pile of the curse questionnaires.

"In case Mrs Sharpe wants us to hand the homework in, as well as telling her about it." She put one questionnaire in front of the toad. "Do you want help filling it in?"

But the toad just squatted in the middle of the paper and stayed silent.

So Molly sat at a desk in the corner and wrote down the one-word answers that summarised her interview with Mr Crottel.

No, no and no.

It didn't look very positive.

But she did write Yes under one question: *Do you deserve to be free of this curse?*

Then she said, "Innes, I know you think your dad deserved to be cursed, but you have written down that *you* deserve to be free of it, haven't you?"

Innes held his sheet out to her and she saw a firm dark YES under the eleventh question.

Molly looked at the toad. "I wonder what you did to be cursed. Did you do something awful, or daft, or brave, or is your curse someone else's fault entirely? You can't tell us any of that, but you can tell us if you think you deserve to be free of your curse."

The toad croaked once, loudly and firmly.

Molly nodded. "So, we can all answer that last question for Mrs Sharpe."

Then they sat quietly at their desks, with their homework in front of them, looking up at the clock above the blackboard. As the hands clicked round to 7 p.m., Mrs Sharpe opened the door.

"You harvested that field wonderfully fast. I wonder how many tatties you'll howk tomorrow? Perhaps not quite so many, if you don't get any sleep tonight... How did you get on with your homework?"

Everyone started to talk at once.

Beth said, "That witch's curse destroys so many trees and..."

Atacama said, "I still don't know who cast..."

The toad croaked.

Innes said, "My father finally admitted..."

Molly said, "I think Mr Crottel wants me to *die* as a hare..."

Mrs Sharpe held her hands up. "Shhhh. Perhaps I should read the answers rather than hear them." She walked round the desks, picking up the homework sheets. "What neat handwriting, Innes. Molly, how nice of you to do Beth's sheet as well. And Innes scribed for Atacama. It's lovely to see you all getting along so well!" She folded the sheets and dropped them in her apron pocket. "Now, your next task—"

"But don't you want to read our homework right now?" asked Innes.

"The answers were for you, not for me. You must all understand your own curses. I'll glance at these tonight, over a mug of hogweed tea. But now, I have another task for you: a curse to consider."

"One of our curses?" asked Beth.

"No, a different curse. I'll give you the same information about this curse as you've discovered about your own curses, then you can consider whether it's possible for you to lift this old curse. I also want you to consider the consequences of lifting a curse and whether it is wise to lift every single curse. Then I want you to get out there into the night, as a team, and do what you think is best."

She opened the cupboard Molly had just been looking in, pulled out one of the scrolls, unrolled the top and peered at it, then nodded. She laid the scroll on the desk at the front. "Tonight's homework. There's a hot meal in the bunkhouse, and you can pop into the shop after breakfast tomorrow to let me know how you got on."

She smiled at them and left the barn, the door banging gently behind her.

Molly looked at the clock on the wall. "That was two minutes. She was in here for two minutes. Can she really teach us how to lift our curses in two minutes a day? She didn't even seem that interested in all the homework we did. I thought she'd be a bit more hands-on."

"I didn't," muttered Beth. "Witches do as little as possible. Enchanted brooms to clean the house. Eternal fire to cook the food. Cursed children to howk the tatties. Of course we have to learn about curses all on our own..."

Innes said, "Don't be so negative. She's getting us to do practical tasks, rather than just copying down notes."

Atacama said in his purring calming voice. "Shall we read about our next task first or eat the meal first?"

"Both at the same time," said Innes, seizing the scroll and pushing open the door. "Come on, quickly, let's get a move on."

Beth sighed. "He was less tiring when he was in a bad mood."

Molly ladled out bean stew while Innes cut thick slices of bread. Atacama and Beth bent their black and purple heads

over the scroll, moving the toad down the parchment as they examined each question and answer.

"It's a cursed wyrm," said Beth. "Trapped inside the hill at Cut Rigg Farm, southeast of here, towards the mountains. The wyrm accidentally destroyed the farmhouse and barn. It coiled round the farm buildings one night, squeezed its coils as it slept and knocked down the walls."

"A worm?" asked Molly. "A worm big enough to knock down a wall?"

"Not an earthworm," said Innes, wiggling his forefinger. "A wyrm – W-Y-R-M – a serpent. A great long strong serpent, with a few frills and a bit of a brain. They usually keep away from towns, villages and farms."

"So, did the farmer curse this… wyrm?"

"Yes," said Beth. "Decades ago. When it was cursed, it sank into the earth, and it will stay there, coiled up asleep round the ruins, until someone lifts the curse."

"And is that someone us?" asked Molly. "Do we really want to set a big serpent free?"

"Let's find out if it's possible to set it free first," said Innes.

"The wyrm will awaken," said Atacama, reading from the scroll, "when the farm is rebuilt in one night, just as it was destroyed in one night. If the wyrm uncoils itself and moves off the farm's land without knocking down one stone of the building, the curse will be lifted and the wyrm will be free."

"So," said Innes, cutting more bread and putting it beside the toad, "we have to rebuild a farm tonight."

"But do we?" asked Molly. "Mrs Sharpe said this was about deciding whether it's wise to lift a curse, not just barging ahead and lifting it anyway. Does it say whether the curse is deserved?"

Beth pushed the parchment towards Molly.

Molly looked at the answers under the familiar questions. "It says the curse was possibly a little out of proportion, because the farmhouse was newly inherited and the owner was very fond of it." She frowned. "But this doesn't have the 'deserve to be free' question. And there isn't a question about the consequences of lifting the curse. We didn't have to think about the consequences of lifting our own curses either. But maybe that's a question we should ask. What would happen if we let a wyrm loose in Speyside? Are wyrms dangerous? What do they eat? Might it attack us when we wake it up?"

"Wyrms mostly eat cattle and sheep, but they digest slowly so they don't eat that often," said Innes, dipping a crust in his stew. "I'm sure we'll be safe while it's cold and groggy from waking up."

Beth added, "It won't stay round here long anyway, once it realises the witch who cursed it still lives nearby."

"Where?" asked Molly.

"Look at the name on the sheet."

Molly looked at the answer to the very first question. "Oh. Aggie Sharpe. It was Mrs Sharpe who cursed the wyrm? That was her farm? She wants us to lift her own curse?"

"Looks like it," said Innes, "so let's get on with it."

Molly sighed. She wasn't sure they'd done what Mrs Sharpe asked and really considered the consequences of lifting this curse. She looked round the table. Innes was eating his second bowl of stew, the toad was squatting on its slice of bread, Beth was filling glasses of water for everyone, Atacama was nibbling a bit of red pepper. Everyone looked calm and unafraid. They knew far more about the world of magic and spells and curses, the world that contained wyrms, than Molly did. If they didn't think freeing a giant serpent was a problem, maybe it wasn't.

Molly was the stranger here, the one who didn't fit in, and she didn't want to ask any more awkward questions. And surely Mrs Sharpe wouldn't have given them this task if it was dangerous.

She shrugged. "Alright, let's build a farm."

Atacama said, "Building a farmhouse and outbuildings in one night won't be as easy as digging tatties."

"I can manage any woodwork," said Beth.

Innes said, "I can do stonework, in my horse self. Humans used to capture and bridle kelpies to force them to work at building or hauling or ploughing, because we're so strong, and because all manual work goes faster when kelpies are involved. If I work willingly, without a bridle or coercion, and you all work with me, we can do this in one night."

Atacama smiled at Molly. "You and I will be labourers for the dryad and kelpie tonight."

"What will the toad do?"

"I'm sure the toad will be very useful, if the toad cares to come along..."

The toad leapt off the slightly squashed bread and walked towards the door.

As everyone grabbed their coats, hats and scarves, Molly found a clean fleece, then they all went outside. Molly and Beth wheeled the bikes out of the shed and Beth put the toad in her basket.

Innes yawned. "I need a gallop after all that digging." Then he changed into a horse.

At the corner of the shed, he just changed into a horse.

Molly watched carefully. He didn't stretch or go through transition shapes of part-boy part-horse. The shift was simple and elegant. He was a boy. Then the air and light swirled round him, he was indistinct for a moment, and when he came back into focus, he was a horse.

Molly turned to Beth. "Is that what it looks like when I change?"

"I don't know," said Beth. "I haven't been paying attention. Ask Innes. He's an expert on the finer points of shapeshifting."

"I can't really ask him now..." Molly turned to the tall white stallion, and reached out to stroke his nose. Then she remembered the horse was Innes and she wouldn't stroke his nose when he was a boy. Or an underwater monster, or a pike. So she just smiled and said, "Will you tell me later whether I change the same way you do?"

The horse nodded, then galloped off, followed by the long shadowy shape of the sphinx.

Molly said, "Couldn't Atacama fly there?"

"No, his wings are just for show," replied Beth. "They're not strong enough to lift his weight off the ground. Only sphinx kittens actually fly. Come on." And she cycled off into the dark.

Chapter Thirteen

Molly thought they were pedalling up slopes far more often than coasting down, so they must be cycling into the hills. She wondered if she'd have the energy to do any building once they got to the farm. Perhaps the wyrm had only knocked down a few stones. Perhaps it wouldn't be much work at all...

When Beth shouted, "We're nearly there," they pulled the bikes off the road into a ditch. Beth stood at the bottom of a narrow track between two fenced-off fields and called, "Hello? Innes, Atacama?"

Molly heard Innes's distant voice. "Up here. Bring the lights from your bikes."

Beth said, "I can do better than that." She found a branch lying on the verge and whispered to it. The end of the branch burst into flame, making a sudden bright torch in her hand.

Molly lifted the toad out of the basket and they followed the steep track up the hill. Atacama was laughing when they arrived. "Poor Innes having to ask for light. None of his eyes are as good in the dark as my cat's eyes."

Innes, who was leaning against a fence in his boy form, said, "I had to go slow for you on the way here, because my horse legs are better than your cat paws."

"Have your clever cat's eyes noticed any trees round here?" asked Beth.

Atacama said, "Down by the road, just beyond where you left the bikes."

Beth ordered, "Right, everyone give me a hand."

As they traipsed back down the hill, Atacama said, "I saw three buildings: a small farmhouse, a bigger but simpler barn and a little outhouse."

"And they're all completely tumbled down," added Innes. "I tripped over what's left of the barn. It's very low to the ground and the stones are scattered everywhere. It's a full night's work, even with a kelpie."

Beth led them into a small dark gathering of trees, creaky with sleepy bird noises above their heads. "We'll need lots of branches for lights, scaffolding and a simple hurdle for Innes to haul stone. So I want every branch and every twig you can find piled up here. But only fallen wood, hare-girl, don't you dare break a limb of any living tree."

"I know..." said Molly.

Beth leant forward and murmured to the trees.

At first, in the dark, Molly could only find branches by stumbling over them. But once Beth had finished speaking to the trees, she lit more torches and stuck them in the ground, so gathering wood was much easier. The toad even dragged some twigs over to Beth.

They built a bonfire-sized pile of wood very quickly. Molly wondered whether it was because work goes faster with a kelpie involved.

"What about a strong plank," asked Beth, "for a lever or catapault system?"

"That would be useful," Innes agreed, shouting to be heard over the increasing volume of sleepy birds rustling and croaking above their heads.

"Keep your voices down," said Beth. "This must be the crows' roosting site and we're disturbing their sleep. I saw a wooden gate a few hundred metres back. Innes, you and the hare-girl take that apart and bring the longest strongest plank. I'll put it back together later."

Molly and Innes walked out of the trees and followed the fence along the roadside.

"Won't the farm animals escape if we break the gate?" asked Molly.

"I galloped through this field earlier. It's empty. There's nothing around here but us, a sleeping wyrm and those grumpy crows."

Molly shoved a burning torch into the ground and looked at the sturdy wooden gate: three horizontal planks and one longer plank nailed diagonally across them.

"How are we going to take it apart? I don't have a hammer or a screwdriver."

Innes laughed. "I have hooves!"

And he shifted.

Molly watched more closely this time. There definitely

weren't any intermediate stages. He was a boy, there was a moment when she couldn't quite focus on him, then he was a horse.

The shining white horse swung round and kicked twice. Once at the bottom corner of the diagonal plank and once at the top corner. The gate sagged, the planks hanging crookedly from bent nails.

Innes changed back again, in the same cloudy unfocussed way, and said, "Let's pull out the nails and ease the longest plank free."

"Is that how I change?" Molly asked, as she tugged on a loose nail at the top corner. "A girl, a cloudy moment, then a hare? Is that what it seems like to you?"

"No," said Innes, crouching down at the bottom corner. "I've only seen you shift a couple of times, but it's not the same as when I watch my family shift. It looks more violent for you, more of a collapse inwards or an explosion outwards. How does it feel?"

"Hot. A flash of heat in my bones. But only for a moment, then I'm fine to run."

Innes stood up and started pulling on the diagonal plank. "When I shift, it feels like taking a step sideways. It's comfy and natural, because the horse, the pike and this boy are all part of who I am. But you aren't meant to change shape. It's been forced on you; it's not part of your nature."

"Is it damaging me?" She looked at her hands, thinking how much smaller they were when she was a hare and how much pressure she put on them as she sprinted and leapt.

Innes shrugged. "Probably not. I'm not an expert on other shapeshifters, but if it was damaging you permanently, I'm sure Mrs Sharpe would be advising you to keep away from dogs, instead of sending you to interview the dog-dirt chucker. It might not be doing you any harm, but it's not how you're meant to live."

He jerked the plank free. They walked awkwardly away from the drooping gate, one at each end of the long heavy plank, watching their feet for rabbit holes and cowpats, calling out: "left" "right" "slower" and "watch out for that huge squishy one".

As they headed towards the patch of trees, they saw light flickering through the tree trunks and heard crows squawking and shrieking.

"We'd better help Beth get the sticks out of there, so those birds can go back to sleep," said Innes.

But as they got closer, they could see crows diving at Beth and Atacama.

Innes dropped the plank and ran to the trees.

Molly started dragging the plank herself, not bothering about whether she was trailing it through cowpats.

"I don't know!" she heard Beth shouting. "Perhaps they didn't like the torchlight? Let's get out and leave them alone."

Molly saw that the wood had been piled onto a sort of sledge made of branches woven tightly together, like a trailer without wheels. She hefted the plank onto the edge of the pile, then ducked as a dark shape swooped at her head.

Innes was already a horse and Beth was looping a rope of twisted bark round his pale neck. Then, just like a plough horse in an old painting, Innes hauled the pile of wood up the hill, away from the annoyed crows.

Beth said, "Molly, help me get the torches."

Molly ran into the trees and pulled up four torches, then held them carefully in a flaming bundle.

Beth called, "Sorry to disturb you, my feathered friends. We'll leave you to roost in peace now." They followed the horse and the sphinx towards the tumbledown ruin.

"Where's the toad?" asked Molly.

"Perched on top of the load," gasped Beth. "Guarding a couple of twigs he was very proud of."

"Did you make that sledge thing?"

Beth nodded, her face clear in the light of the half dozen torches she was carrying. "It's a hurdle, used for pulling loads on rough ground."

"How did you make it so fast?"

"I asked the wood to twist and weave, and showed it how."

"But wasn't the fallen wood dead?"

"Not completely. All wood has a little life energy left in it and I can call on that, to create light or warmth or a new shape. We're woodworkers as well as tree spirits."

"That's useful," said Molly. "Maybe we *will* get this done in one night."

"If you pull your weight, hare-girl, we might. Don't slow us down." Beth marched off.

Molly sighed. She couldn't even give that girl a compliment without annoying her.

When Molly reached the farm, Beth was pushing torches into the ground. But Molly didn't see three buildings, she just saw heaps of stone.

How could they rebuild this in a night?

Then she noticed Atacama shoving at the back of the hurdle, trying to get it over a steep rise. She jabbed her handful of torches into the ground in a bright jumble, then lifted the edge of the hurdle and eased it over the hump.

"Why didn't you just go round this?" she asked.

"Because it rings the farm," said Atacama.

Molly stood on the highest point of the small ridge and saw that it circled round the ruins. Like earthworks round ancient standing stones or the edge of a moat round a castle.

"Why would a farm have...?" Then she stopped. "Is this the wyrm?"

Beth laughed. "Yes. Of course."

Molly jumped down and took a few fast steps away from the ring of grass and heather.

Beth laughed even louder. "Don't be scared, hare-girl. It's sound asleep. And it won't wake up until we build these walls."

Chapter Fourteen

"Remember why we're doing this." Innes stood on the tumbledown wall, a blazing torch in each hand. "It's not about the farm, it's not about the wyrm, it's about us and our curses. This is a task to prove ourselves to Mrs Sharpe. If we work as a team, rebuild the farm, free the wyrm and return with our homework done, then she'll lift our curses. So, here's what we do."

He held the torches out wide, pointing both ways along the ruined wall. "This is the farmhouse. It will need a chimney, windows, a door. The barn, over there," he swung the torches so fast that sparks flew, "is bigger, but simpler, so it won't take as long. We'll leave the outhouse until last and build it from leftover stones.

"First, Atacama and I will haul the stones into graded piles, while Beth, Molly and the toad build scaffolding. Then we'll create a catapult system, to get the stones from the ground to the walls."

"What about cement?" asked Molly. "To hold the stones in place?"

Innes laughed. "We won't need cement. With a kelpie at work, every stone will stay where we put it!"

Molly muttered to Beth, "He's confident."

Beth said, "We each have our own skills and powers, there's no point being modest about them. You're definitely best at lying still and running away."

Molly bit back a reply, and took a step away to look at the size of the house.

"Mind the toad!" Beth yelled.

Molly looked down. Her heel was pressing into the ground just millimetres from the toad's head. "Sorry, toad." She moved her foot. "So, Beth, can I help build the scaffolding?"

"No. Only dryads can talk to wood. You can fetch and carry for me. I'll build a tower against this wall, then we'll move it round when we want to build the next one."

So they took off their coats and scarves, and rolled up their sleeves. Atacama and Innes used the hurdle to gather the stones scattered around the hillside. Beth built a tall wooden structure with the branches Molly and the toad brought her.

"Pass me up the brightest torch," Beth called, as she clambered up the scaffolding.

Molly hesitated. "Isn't putting burning branches on wooden scaffolding a fire risk?"

Beth reached her hand down. "My torches will burn only what I ask them to burn."

Molly pulled a torch from the ground and reached up with it. But she couldn't stretch far enough. "Give me a minute, I'll climb up with it."

"No need," said Beth, "just let go."

"Really?"

"Really! If you question all my instructions, we'll never finish in a night. You're always slowing us down, hare-girl."

Molly took a deep breath. "I know you don't like me, Beth, and I've been ignoring your snarky comments because we're all trying to work together, but I'm running out of patience. So, honestly, if you can't be polite, I'll go and help Innes and Atacama, then we'll see how long it takes you to build scaffolding with just a toad to boss about."

She stared at Beth.

Beth glared at her.

Then Beth said, "Let go of the torch, *please*."

Molly nodded, let go of the torch and ducked out of the way, expecting it to fall.

But the torch didn't fall.

The torch rose, through the air, to Beth's outstretched hand. Beth grabbed it, and tied it with bark twine to the scaffolding.

Molly turned to the toad, who was dragging a twig over. "Wow. She can do anything with wood. Even ignore gravity."

The toad croaked. Which was either a yes, or a complaint at the weight of the twig.

After building one more layer of wooden scaffolding they were ready to start the stone walls.

Molly, Beth, Atacama and the toad stood on the lowest

level of the scaffolding, watching Innes the boy put a stone on one end of what looked like a seesaw, then change to Innes the horse and stamp a heavy hoof on the other end. The stone flew into the air in a precise curve and landed on the top edge of the wall.

Innes called up, "Is that stone secure?"

The stone was sitting slightly squint, so Molly eased it into place, and called down, "This one's fine, send up the next." Another stone curved up, to thump into the next space on the wall.

"Watch out!" Beth yelled at Atacama. "You nearly knocked the toad off the scaffolding with your tail!"

Atacama said, "This isn't the safest place for you, is it, toad? Why don't you start building the outhouse yourself, and we'll help after we've finished the larger buildings?"

Once the toad jumped down, they moved more confidently on the tower.

Soon, Innes was sending up stones so fast that Beth, Molly and Atacama were kept busy straightening the stones, first on the lower level, then the middle level of the scaffolding.

When Molly climbed to the highest level of the scaffolding to get ready for the next layer of stones, she saw something move at the edge of her vision. Something black and glossy in the wavering torchlight.

At first she thought it was Atacama, climbing up to help her. But this shape wasn't sinuous, it was jerky.

She saw it move closer.

A crow.

The crow strode across the scaffolding, its beak jabbing into the air with each strutting step, then perched on the wall.

"Innes, stop!" Molly shouted. "Don't send another stone up yet. There's a crow here, and you'll crush it!"

In a fluttering of shiny feathers, more crows settled on the pale stones.

Molly said softly, "Sorry if we've woken you up, but that's not a safe place to roost. Please go back to your comfy trees." But they didn't move.

Molly called down, "Does anyone speak crow? We have a problem..."

"What kind of problem?" Beth scrambled up.

Molly pointed at the line of crows. "I think they're staging a sit-down protest, to stop us building any higher. Can you persuade them to go away?"

"How? I can't talk to crows."

"You talk to trees!"

"I'm a tree spirit. I'm not a crow spirit. I can't talk to crows or mice or midgies or anything else that isn't magical and doesn't use words."

Molly leant down. "Atacama? Do you speak crow?"

The sphinx jumped up beside her. "I don't speak to birds." He smiled. "I eat birds." He took a step towards the crows.

They didn't move.

"Don't hurt them!" said Beth.

"I'm not trying to hurt them. I'm trying to persuade them they'd be safer somewhere else." He took a slow low stalking-predator step towards the line of a dozen crows.

They looked calmly back at him. They didn't move.

Innes clambered up and squeezed between Molly and Beth. "On three, everyone shout and wave and flap and pretend to be a scary scarecrow. 1, 2, 3..."

On the narrow platform, Atacama roared and reared and pawed the air, while Innes, Beth and Molly yelled and clapped and flapped their arms.

One small crow at the end of the line opened its beak and cawed, *kraa-ha-ha-ha-ha-ha*, but the crows didn't move.

The scaffolding moved though, wobbling under their feet.

"Stop," said Innes. "They're not easily frightened."

Beth knelt down and murmured to the shoogly wooden frame. Once Beth had steadied the scaffolding, they sat down carefully, backs to the crows, looking out into the dark night.

"Perhaps this is a test," said Atacama. "Are we prepared to hurt innocent crows to free the wyrm?"

"Of course not," said Beth.

"I'm a hunter," said Innes. "I don't have the same attitude to hurting non-magical creatures as you. But if this is a test set by Mrs Sharpe, then we shouldn't hurt these crows deliberately, even if they are being really annoying. So how can we build the walls?"

"Maybe we shouldn't build them," said Molly. "We still haven't properly discussed whether it's sensible or wise to free this wyrm. We already know that a freed wyrm might eat local sheep and cows and who knows what else, and now building these walls might injure the crows. Mrs Sharpe didn't tell us to lift the curse, she told us to consider whether we *should* lift it. I think *that's* the test."

Innes sighed. "But if we don't free the wyrm, it seems like we're wimping out. I don't like wimping out. If we can find a way to lift the curse without hurting the crows, that would show teamwork and commitment to the workshop."

Molly asked, yet again, "So no one else thinks setting a huge serpent free is risky?"

Beth laughed. "You really are a hare-girl, aren't you? Scared of everything! It's not *that* risky. The wyrm will probably only take one sheep from one farm once a year. That's far fewer sheep than human cars and lorries kill driving too fast along these roads. I respect life, but predators are part of life, and if we're working with these two predators," she waved at Innes and Atacama, "we can't be squeamish about letting another predator loose."

Molly looked at Innes and Atacama. They both smiled at her with their bright white teeth.

Molly shifted round and looked at the crows. They all stared back at her.

"We can't scare them away," said Molly. "And we don't want to squash them."

"We might *want* to squash them," muttered Innes, "but it wouldn't be wise..."

Molly said, "So let's move them."

"Move them? How?"

"Just pick them up, and put them on the scaffolding rather than the stones."

Innes laughed. "You want to pick up a crow in your bare hands? Do you hear this, Beth? Molly's not scared of everything after all!"

Molly stood up and faced the crows, wondering if it was possible to lift one up without getting her eyes pecked out.

She darted forward and snatched the smallest crow, the one that had laughed at them. She wrapped her hands round its smooth body and wings, and lifted. The crow weighed almost nothing, like it was made of air.

It squawked angrily and jerked about, thrashing its wings, but Molly held tight, carried it over to a wooden rail and gently placed it down. The bird balanced on the rail, preened an out-of-place feather, then turned its head slowly to look at Molly. The gleaming black eyes stared at her face, then the crow jerked its head forward and stabbed at her right hand with its sharp black beak.

Molly yelled and jumped away.

Then all the crows on the wall flew straight at Molly, diving and scratching and stabbing.

Molly fell to the wooden floor of the scaffolding and wrapped her hands around her head. But the crows kept mobbing her, whacking with their wings, striking with their beaks, tearing with their claws.

Molly tried not to scream as she heard Atacama snarling above her and felt the crows flapping away from her.

When she looked up, the crows were sitting calmly on the wall again.

Molly shuffled to the far edge of the scaffolding. "This isn't a passive protest any more." She clenched her fists to stop her hands trembling. "They really don't want us to build here – and they're willing to hurt us."

Innes grabbed Molly's hand and looked at the blood on her skin. He turned to the crows. "I don't know if you're ordinary crows or something else. And I don't really care. We are building this farm tonight and if you get in our way, or hurt my friends again, then I will hurt you."

All the crows launched themselves towards him, diving at his face.

Innes laughed and jumped backwards off the scaffolding. The crows flew after him. The other three looked down and saw the white horse on the ground, kicking at black crows with his hooves.

Atacama said, "If Innes can send stones up, I'll settle them in place."

Beth nodded. "Hare-girl, can you use a torch to keep the crows away from Innes down there, while I keep them off Atacama up here?"

"Of course." Molly wiped her bloody hands on her jeans, then clambered down the scaffolding.

Innes was rearing and bucking and kicking, as the crows mobbed him, screaming their short harsh barking calls.

"Don't worry about the crows!" Molly grabbed a torch from the ground. "Just concentrate on sending the stones up."

She waved the torch in the air, whirling it round, driving the crows away from Innes.

He shifted into a boy and dragged a stone onto one end of his plank. Then he shifted into a horse and stamped on the other end.

Molly swung the torch, forcing the crows away from Innes as he sent stones up so fast that he was a blur of boy and horse.

Molly and the crows moved fast too. The birds kept diving at Innes, and she kept sweeping them away with the torch. She didn't set fire to any feathers with her flames, but she got close enough to keep them wary. She was dancing round the kelpie, tripping over the pile of coats and scarves, leaping over the empty hurdle.

The crows didn't give up: half a dozen were attacking Innes and half a dozen were attacking Atacama. But the girls' effective defence with the torches meant the crows couldn't stop the kelpie and the sphinx building, so the wall grew taller, layer on layer.

Then Beth called down, "We've finished the south wall, we'll have to move the scaffolding round to the—"

But her voice was drowned out by a vast vibrating shriek. Not from the crows attacking them, but from the sky above. It sounded like hundreds of crows shrieking together – or one huge crow giving an order.

Suddenly a black blizzard of feathers fell on them from the sky.

Each of them was being attacked by dozens of crows.

Molly, who had been chasing away small numbers of crows easily with swings of the torch, found herself being mobbed by so many crows that she couldn't aim at them all at once.

Then one crow grasped her right wrist and another pecked viciously at her hand.

Molly dropped the torch.

Now she had nothing to defend herself or Innes with.

Molly crouched low to the ground, covering her face and her eyes. She was being bombarded by wings and claws and beaks.

She could hear Innes bellowing and stamping his hooves. She could hear Atacama roaring high above her. She could hear Beth screaming.

She could hear herself screaming too. She was covered in crows, all pecking and scratching.

Molly crawled towards the pile of coats, hoping to shelter under them. Her knee banged into something smooth and wooden. The hurdle that Beth had woven. It felt flimsy but it had held massive weights of wood and stone. Could it protect her?

She moved her hands away from her face to pull the hurdle up and over herself. But above the clouds of crows that were attacking Innes, she saw something larger than a bird.

She saw Beth rising into the air.

Dozens of crows had grabbed the dryad's dark clothes in their black claws and beaks, and were lifting her off the scaffolding.

Beth yelled, "Help! They're going to drop me! *Help!*"

The crows flew upwards, lifting Beth higher and higher...

Chapter Fifteen

Beth screamed in panic as the crows flew her into the night sky. Atacama and Innes yelled threats. Molly didn't shout, or even stand up. She was trembling too much. Perhaps she really was a hare-girl, scared of everything.

But however scared she was of the crows attacking her, she couldn't cower under a hurdle while Beth was in danger. She shoved the hurdle away with her bleeding right hand, so she wouldn't be tempted to hide.

As she pushed it, she felt the rough bark and twisted twigs of the fallen wood. Wood that still contained some life energy, Beth had said. Wood that would use that energy for Beth, if Beth asked.

But Beth couldn't ask, because she was being flown to her death. Could someone else ask the wood for her?

"Innes?" Molly croaked. "Innes? Can you talk to wood?"

But the kelpie couldn't hear her, as he changed between a boy shouting and a horse kicking, then back again.

So Molly crawled forward on her belly, her covering

of crows pecking and whacking her, and she placed her bleeding right hand on the edge of the hurdle. "Please," she whispered. "I'm not a dryad, but Beth is. I don't want her to get hurt or killed when the crows drop her."

Molly could see crows releasing Beth's clothes and hair, one by one. She patted the hurdle, wondering how to wake it up, accidentally smearing her blood on the woven wood.

"Please. I know there's still life in you. And I've seen how much Beth cares about her trees. Please, wood, if you can move like you used to move in the wind, please catch Beth when they drop her."

She looked up. More crows were letting go. Beth was now held by no more than a couple of dozen birds, who could barely carry her weight.

Molly gasped, "Please, branches and twigs and bark. Please! Save Beth. Save the dryad."

The hurdle quivered under her fingers. She lifted her hand away.

The hurdle rose off the ground, then the rectangle of woven wood sliced through the air, aiming for the empty space under Beth.

The last few crows let go.

Beth screamed as she fell.

The hurdle flew under her and she landed hard on the wood. Beth grapped the edges of the hurdle, as it spun out of control, and tumbled towards the ground.

Molly saw Beth speak to the woven twigs, then the hurdle slowed its dive. It floated gently down to land

exactly where it had been when Molly asked it to help.

Innes yelled, "Under cover, everyone, under the hurdle."

Beth stumbled off the hurdle, then dragged it up against the newly built wall, under the first level of scaffolding. The sphinx, the kelpie, the dryad and the girl all squashed under it, Atacama snarling and biting at any crows who tried to follow them.

Now, with the wall on one side, the hurdle canted above, and all of them facing inwards so the crows were flapping at their backs, not their faces, Molly felt almost safe.

"Are you ok, Beth?" asked Innes.

"I'm scratched and shaking, but I'm fine. Is everyone else ok?"

They nodded.

"What about the toad?" asked Molly.

"There are plenty of dark corners near the outhouse, so if the toad had time to hide, I'm sure it will be safe," said Atacama. "And if the toad isn't hiding, it's too late for us to help."

No one said anything for a moment.

Then Innes spoke. "So. We're all dying to know, Molly. What in the name of the good green earth did you just do?"

"Indeed," purred Atacama. "Are you really a magical being, hiding behind pretended human ignorance?"

"No, I just put my hand on the hurdle and asked it politely to save Beth. I explained that Beth was a dryad and needed help. I asked nicely and it did what I asked."

"Wow," said Innes. "You just *asked*?"

"I asked *nicely.*"

"With that hand on the wood?" Atacama stroked her right wrist with his soft black paw.

She nodded.

Beth said, "Did you say you were my friend and that's why the wood helped?"

"No. You haven't treated me like a friend and I didn't think lying would work. So I just said you needed help."

Beth looked away. "Thank you."

"Perhaps it was the blood," said Atacama. "If you bled on the wood and asked selflessly for someone in mortal danger, both of those actions are powerful spells. Friendship is another powerful magic, but you didn't need to call on that too."

"Next time you *can* call on friendship," said Beth. "I know I can be as prickly as a bramble and as rude as a rhododendron, and I know I haven't hidden my dislike of humans interfering in our world, but you saved me, Molly. I'm sorry I've never been as polite to you as you were to the wood. And I'd be proud to call you my friend."

Beth held out her hand and Molly shook it.

Innes said, "Isn't that nice and cosy and sickly sweet? Now we're all friends. All except the crows, who really don't want us to build this farm. So who has powers that can fight them off?"

"Shapeshifting won't help," said Beth. "Unless either of you can shift into an eagle and fight them in the air."

"I'm land and water only," said Innes.

"I can just do a hare," said Molly, "and I can't even control that."

"Beth's torches defended us against the smaller flock of crows," said Atacama. "Could we use lots more torches, to scare off lots more crows?"

"We don't have enough hands for lots more torches," said Beth.

"We don't need hands," said Molly. "You can control wood in the air. You floated a torch up the scaffolding."

Innes asked, "Could you persuade all the wood you're not using for scaffolding to whirl around and whack the crows off us? Could you make us a shield?"

She shrugged. "I suppose I could create a barrier of moving sticks to keep the crows out of the worksite, with a few torches to deter them even more. But it would take a lot of effort, and I'd need to concentrate on the wood. I couldn't build at the same time."

"That's fine. If you protect us, I'll send stones up, and Atacama and Molly can settle them in place. We can finish before dawn if you all work at kelpie speed..."

So Beth built a small shield of airborne sticks, and expanded it branch by branch until it covered the house, then the barn, then the whole site. Soon the team were completely covered by a dome of whirling wood and flaming torches, safe in the crow-free area underneath, listening to the angry cawing of crows outside.

Molly called, "Toad, if you can hear me, you can come out now!" But there was no answer.

So Beth sat cross-legged on the highest wall, murmuring and chanting to the sticks that were spinning above her head. Molly and Innes moved the scaffolding and the plank round, then Innes started flicking stones up again, while Molly and Atacama shoved them into place.

They found a fast and efficient rhythm, and built the walls high and strong.

"We should use a kelpie to build all the time," Molly said as they moved the scaffolding round the next corner. She had to yell to be heard over the clacking of sticks and the screeching of crows.

"This is why humans forced us to build for them," Innes called back. "But your ministers and lairds didn't ask nicely. They forced kelpies to build fancy houses by stealing kelpie children and threatening them. Ministers preached against belief in magic while their manses were being built by labour stolen from magical creatures. So most kelpies don't like to build, it brings back memories of those old stories."

He looked up at the new walls. "But this is quite fun: building for a good reason, with people I like."

He pointed to a gap in the line of stones on the ground. "This is the wall with the door. I'll build a doorframe and lintel as I send the stones over."

So they built a wall with a door and windows almost as fast as the other walls. Soon the farmhouse was built and the barn half-built too.

"What about the roofs?" asked Molly, as they were

moving the scaffolding round for the last time. She rubbed her shoulders. She could feel the work she'd been doing in the stiffness of her muscles, but she wasn't tired.

Innes frowned. "We'll need Beth and her wood for the roofs. Perhaps the crows will give up and go away by the time we've finished the stonework, so she can let the barrier down."

But the crows didn't give up. As Innes, Molly and Atacama built the last wall of the barn, they could still hear the birds screeching and see the occasional tattered black feather fall through the barrier of whirling burning wood.

When both the main buildings were finished, they walked round the barn to start on the outhouse, which Molly assumed had been the farm's toilet.

But the outhouse was already complete. A building no bigger than a bus stop, with four walls, a doorway and a roof. And the toad squatting in front of it.

Molly ran over. "I'm so glad the crows didn't attack you! Are you alright?"

The toad croaked once.

"Did you finish this yourself?"

The toad croaked again.

"Well done. How did you do it?"

The toad was silent.

Molly turned to Innes and Atacama. "Now we have to work out how to build the roofs without leaving ourselves unprotected."

The toad jumped into the outhouse.

"Do you want to shelter in there while we do the other roofs?" asked Innes. "Fair enough, you've done lots of work already."

The toad croaked twice, crawled surprisingly fast out of the shed and round their feet and paws, then back in.

Molly nodded. "The toad wants us all to go in. It's the only completed building. If we use the hurdle as a door, we can all take shelter in there, then we won't need the barrier, so Beth can drop it down onto the house and barn as roofs."

Atacama said, "But Beth will need to come down from the wall into the outhouse, while she's still maintaining the barrier."

"I'll bring her down," said Molly.

Innes said, "I'll fetch the hurdle."

As she and Innes dragged the scaffolding from the barn to the house, she could hear Beth singing to the wood above their heads. The dryad's voice was hoarse, but she was still flattering the wood, keeping the barrier strong. Molly wasn't sure how to get a message to Beth without interrupting that link.

She scrambled up the scaffolding, then pulled herself onto the flat top of the wall, and saw a pale smudge of light on the horizon. The night was nearly over. There was no time to be subtle.

Molly walked along the wall and stood in front of Beth. The dryad looked up at her, and Molly heard the chant become simpler, just a repetition of the seasons.

"We need the wood for roofs."

Beth nodded and spoke a few encouraging words about sap and photosynthesis.

"We all have to shelter in the outhouse."

Beth nodded again and described several different shades of green.

"Come down right now."

Beth stood and stretched, chanting about dancing with the wind.

Molly balanced along the wall to the scaffolding. Beth followed her, murmuring about roots and soil.

As they climbed down, both of them concentrating on footholds and handholds, Beth murmured more slowly and Molly noticed a couple of sticks fall out of the air above her. The barrier was already weakening.

When she and Beth reached the ground, she heard a caw of triumph and looked up to see a stream of crows pushing through a small gap in the barrier.

"RUN!"

Beth and Molly ran, as sticks clattered down around them, and beaks and claws crashed into them.

Molly dragged Beth, who was wobbly and barely whispering about twigs and buds, round the barn to the outhouse. She shoved Beth through the outhouse doorway and fell in after her. Innes blocked the gap with the hurdle and Atacama held it in place with his claws.

"Here we are again," said Innes. "In a small space, with annoyed crows outside. But this time, we're trapped in a toilet!"

"It's nearly dawn," said Molly. "Beth, how fast can you turn that shield into roofs?"

Beth coughed. "I need to see what I'm doing." Her voice was overwhelmed by the noise of wood crashing down onto the outhouse. The barrier was falling apart.

Atacama moved the hurdle over slightly. Beth put her face to the gap, but she jerked back immediately and a black beak stabbed the air where her face had been. Atacama slammed the hurdle back over the doorway.

"If I look, they'll peck out my eyes; if I don't, I can't build the roofs..." The dryad was shivering, though Molly couldn't tell whether it was from the sudden fright or with exhaustion from maintaining the barrier.

Innes said, "Beth, you know where the walls are, because you've been sitting on top of them. You know every stick out there personally. You don't need to see. And if I help, you can call on my kelpie work rate for speed and efficiency."

Atacama said, "It's less than ten minutes until dawn. We have to do this *now*."

Innes sat down and pulled Beth down with him. He held both her hands and said gently, "I'm going to describe the buildings and you're going to place your wood on top to make the best roofs ever built in five minutes. You can do this."

Atacama, Molly and the toad watched in the dim torchlight, as Innes described the walls' dimensions and Beth murmured to her wood. Soon there were caws of frustration outside, almost masking the calm whispering of the kelpie and the dryad, but not quite covering the firm thumps of wood linking together.

After a few minutes, Beth said, “I think that’s it. But I have to look now, to check if the roofs look right as well as feel right.”

“The roofs are fine,” said Innes. “Listen.”

There was one thunderous screech of anger from the crows, then silence.

“Is it safe?” asked Molly.

Atacama nudged the hurdle over and they looked out cautiously, ready to leap back if any beaks jabbed at them.

But the crows were swooping away to distant trees and fenceposts, and in the faint light of dawn, Molly could see two low wooden roofs on the farm buildings.

“The roofs look perfect!” said Molly. “Well done! And the crows have given up at last.”

She slid the hurdle aside and stepped out. Then she felt the earth move under her feet.

Chapter Sixteen

As Molly stepped away from the outhouse doorway to let the others past, she felt a tickling vibration in the soles of her feet, like mild pins and needles.

Innes burst out of the doorway. "The wyrm is waking! Get out of here! If we're trapped inside its coils, we might be crushed."

He dragged Beth out with him. Molly reached into the outhouse and grabbed the toad.

As they scrambled over the humped ring of earth, where the vibrations felt less tickly and more threatening, Atacama said, "Head for higher ground, so we can watch what happens and keep out of danger."

"Danger?" yelled Molly as she followed the sphinx up the field. "Danger? I kept asking if it was dangerous to set the wyrm free, and you all kept ignoring me, and now you want to run away..."

"This isn't running away," said Innes. "This is a tactical redeployment to a less compromised location. We'll see how big the wyrm is, how sleepy it is, how annoyed it is.

And if it's gigantic, wide awake and angry, *then* we'll run away!"

Finally they leant, gasping, against the fence at the top of the field.

Molly put the toad down, then grinned. "Those look like proper buildings from up here."

Then she noticed that the ridge of earth they had clambered over was a clear circle even from this distance. And the circle was moving.

The ground inside the circle and the ground outside the circle were still and solid, but a ring of land was moving slowly clockwise round the three new buildings. The earth was swirling, like a whirlpool.

"It's waking," said Atacama.

"It's coiling," said Innes.

"It's rising," said Beth.

The toad croaked.

Then the earth started to fracture and fall away. Diamond-shaped fragments of soil fell from the swirling circle.

Molly could see shining lines and zigzags of colour – purples, greens, golds, russets, greys – emerging from the dark brown of the earth.

"Is it just going to stay there, winding round and round?" asked Molly. "Or is it going to..."

A tail flicked up. A long pointed flexible tail ripped up and out of the earth.

"If that's the tail," said Innes, "the head must be..."

And, out of the farmland below them, rose the massive rounded head of the wyrm.

It was bigger than the outhouse they'd been sheltering in five minutes ago.

The wyrm yawned, revealing a forked black tongue and curved white fangs. The space between its jaws was tall enough and wide enough for Innes in his horse form to fit inside.

Then the wyrm turned and looked at them.

Molly stared back.

It was a snake and it wasn't a snake. It was long and legless and scaled, so it looked like a monumentally huge snake. But it wasn't just a snake. It had a frill of skin around its head, where the skull narrowed to the neck. As it looked up the hill, the frill flicked out into a spiny ruff, royal purple and poison yellow, like a frame of swords and silk around its massive mouth and dark gleaming eyes.

It turned to look at the buildings, its head tipping to one side. Then it turned to the south and looked into the wildness of the mountains. The wyrm dragged its thick body out of the trench it had slept in, and began to move away from the farm buildings.

As the wyrm slithered out of the ground, the last clods of earth sliding down its smooth scales, Molly got her first clear look at its markings. It had a zigzag pattern along its body, like lots of Ms nestled into each other, in all the colours of the Scottish landscape, but brighter and shinier.

As it curved across the field, Molly noticed spines

rising up along its backbone. "It's not really a snake, is it? It's almost like a dragon with no legs."

"It *is* a dragon," said Beth. "'Wyrm' is the old word for wingless dragon."

"We just freed a cursed *dragon*?"

"Yes. And now it's leaving." Innes sighed with relief.

There was an echoing shriek like the one they'd heard just before the crows attacked last night. Then hundreds of crows rose from nearby trees and fences, and dived towards the wyrm's head.

The wyrm reared into the air, its head rising higher than the roofs of the buildings, snapping its massive jaws at the crows. The birds wheeled upwards in one smooth motion. The wyrm hissed, lowered its head and started moving away.

The crows swooped down to attack again.

"Should we help it?" asked Beth.

"It might think we're attacking too. We're safer up here," said Atacama.

"Why are they only attacking its left side?" asked Molly.

Innes frowned. "I think they're trying to drive it back to the farm buildings. Why would they…?"

"They're still trying to stop us!" said Atacama. "The curse is only permanently lifted if the wyrm leaves the farm's land without knocking the buildings down again. So the crows are trying to make the wyrm knock a wall down, to stop us lifting the curse…"

"I'm not having those crows wreck our night's work!"

Innes shifted to his horse self and galloped downhill.

Beth said, "We have to guide the wyrm in the other direction." She ran downhill too, swiftly followed by the sphinx.

So Molly scooped the toad up and ran downhill towards a dragon.

The wyrm was no longer heading away in a smooth wave pattern, it was rearing, striking and missing the acrobatic crows, its tail lashing dangerously close to the outhouse.

The crows were harrying and harassing the wyrm, driving it back towards the farm.

But now Innes and Beth were blocking the way to the buildings, waving their arms and shouting.

Molly ran past them, over the new ditch and between the farm buildings. She put the toad down, grabbed the pile of coats and scarves, and ran back.

"Like flags," she said, as she threw them at the others' feet.

"Or red rags to a bull," said Innes.

They all waved the bright colours and yelled, "Get away, go south!"

Now the wyrm was being pecked on one side and yelled at on the other. It writhed and hissed.

The attacking crows kept flying away from its biting jaws, and the yelling children kept jumping away from its whipping tail.

The wyrm snapped at the crows, then whirled round and snapped at Innes. Innes leapt back, falling into the

new ditch, and the head of the wyrm missed him by centimetres.

Then it rose up again and hissed at the crows, as its tail flicked nearer and nearer the newly rebuilt stone walls.

Innes, Beth and Atacama kept shouting, "Go away, go away!"

But Molly yelled, "This isn't working. It's scared and confused. Can it understand what we're saying?"

Innes said, "It's magical: it should understand speech."

So Molly walked out in front of the wyrm and called up, "Wyrm, hello! Wyrm?"

The wyrm opened its huge fanged jaws right above her. Molly saw the dark depths of its mouth descending towards her.

For a cold shivering moment, she forgot why she was standing under this huge monstrous snake. She just watched the tooth-ringed cave open wider and wider.

Then she screamed, "NO! Stop! I'm trying to warn you! I'm trying to save you!"

The wyrm closed its jaws and stared at her.

"The crows want to force you to knock down the buildings, so you'll be trapped under the earth again. Ignore them. Head for the mountains, like you wanted to."

The crows dived down to attack Molly, but she used her fleece like a rotor blade, whirling it above her head to drive them off, and kept her gaze firmly on the wyrm, while it stared back at her with sharp thoughtful eyes.

"We've lifted your curse by rebuilding the farm. But the curse will fall on you again if you knock the walls down. I don't know why these crows care, but they're trying to stop us lifting the curse. Don't let them bully you. Leave carefully and you'll be free..."

The wyrm lowered and raised and lowered its head. Molly wondered if that was a nod.

It hissed once more at the crows, then made a gentle, careful, elegant bend around the outhouse, curved up the field and squeezed its head out through an open gate. It started to slide off into the hills, looking like a piece of land that had been varnished and polished, a perfect s-shaped sliver of Scotland.

The crows wailed.

"Molly, that was insane!" said Beth. "You don't just talk to a wyrm!"

"Why not? You were yelling at it!"

Innes said, "And you certainly don't look directly into a wyrm's eyes!"

"Oh, don't you? Thanks for telling me!"

"Do you feel alright?" asked Beth, putting her hand on Molly's shoulder. "You don't feel... hypnotised or enchanted or be-spelled or anything?"

"No, though I have got these strange voices in my head."

"What voices?" said Innes.

"You lot! Constantly telling me I can't do things when it turns out I can. 'Only dryads can talk to wood', 'It's not safe to look at a wyrm's eyes'. Perhaps you should try breaking your world's rules sometimes, and see what happens..."

There was a sudden silence. The crows had stopped screeching.

Molly looked up. Hundreds of crows were flying slowly in a wide black ring around one solitary crow, which was flapping frantically in the centre of the circle.

As the spiked serpent's tail left the field, the crow in the centre stopped flapping.

The crow fell to the ground, like a black rag.

The other crows circled round once more, then flew off, silently, to the west.

Molly looked at the wyrm sliding off into the hills, then she looked at the dark feathery bundle lying on the grass beyond the ditch.

"At the risk of stating the obvious," said Innes, "I don't think those are ordinary crows."

They crossed the ditch and crouched down by the fallen bird.

Beth reached out and stroked its glossy feathers. "Whether it was ordinary or not, it's dead now. Poor thing."

"Poor thing?" said Innes. "This bird or its friends tried to kill you, and they spent all night trying to stop us completing our task."

"But we did complete our task, and it's dead now. Did we kill it?" Beth laid her hands on the bird and gently stretched out its wings.

In the rising light of the sun, in the iridescent sheen on

the black feathers of the crow's right wing, they saw:

A wyrm.

The glistening image of a wyrm, shining purple and green on the feathers of the bird's wing.

"What is that?" asked Molly.

"It's a link," said Atacama. "I don't know how, but this crow was linked to that wyrm. When the wyrm was set free, the crow died."

"Perhaps the link wasn't to the wyrm, but to the wyrm's curse?" said Beth.

"Is that why they didn't want us to rebuild the farm?" asked Molly. "Because if the curse was lifted, this crow would die?"

"We've freed one creature and killed another," said Beth. "Not as good a night's work as we'd hoped."

"But we've done what Mrs Sharpe asked," said Innes, "so let's go and tell her."

And they all walked away, leaving the crow's body lying crumpled on the ground.

Chapter Seventeen

"I'm tempted to gallop back myself to tell Mrs Sharpe what a bit of kelpie work rate just achieved, but I suppose we should *all* take credit for this successful task," said Innes as they walked back to the bikes. "Atacama and I will wait at the farm gate for you, so we can tell the witch together." He shifted into a horse and galloped off, followed by the loping sphinx.

Beth coiled up the rope she'd made to harness Innes to the hurdle, put it in her bike basket and sat the toad on top. "Innes sharing credit with someone! That's unusual."

Molly said, "He couldn't have done it without us though."

She watched Beth fix the saggy gate with a few firm words, then the two girls cycled back, coasting down the hills. As the slopes flattened out and they reached the richer farmland near the town, Beth said, "Race you to that corner?"

And Molly was beaten again, by a tree riding a bike. She muttered, "I'd be quicker than you on my paws."

Beth smiled. "Would you like me to find a dog and ask it to chase you?"

Molly shivered. "No thanks."

Rounding the next corner, they saw the pale boy and the dark sphinx leaning against the gateposts of Skene Mains Farm as if they'd been waiting for hours.

"Slowcoaches." Innes grinnned.

"We only just got here," said Atacama. "We came the long way round. Innes wanted to stare at a few buildings on the way."

Innes shrugged. "I enjoyed playing with full-sized stone Lego. Maybe we could build something else together after our curses are lifted. A den hut or a team headquarters or..."

"We could build a proper pyramid for Atacama to guard when he gets his riddle back," suggested Beth, wheeling her bike up the lane.

"Or something with lots of fancy roofs for Beth to show off her skills," said Molly. "A castle with towers and domes and pointy bits."

Innes laughed. "That could be a palace for the toad when he turns back into a prince! Or she turns back into a princess..."

"The toad could build a palace himself or herself," said Molly. "Remember the outhouse?"

Innes paused. "It doesn't look like Mrs Sharpe is up. The shop's closed and so are all the farmhouse curtains."

"Let's put the bikes away and have breakfast," said Beth. "We'll tell Mrs Sharpe about the wyrm once she's opened the shop."

The bike shed was locked, so they leant the bikes up against the wall and walked towards the bunkhouse.

"Shhh," said Atacama. "I hear voices." The sphinx led them on soft paws to the back corner of the furthest farm building.

Molly heard Mrs Sharpe's voice, quiet, but clearly angry. "No, Corbie. That's not what we agreed."

All five of them sneaked forward and peered round the corner. They saw Mrs Sharpe talking to a tall man in a long black coat with ragged fingers of fabric dangling down from the sleeves' cuffs and hems.

She said again, "That's not what we agreed."

The man spoke in a rough croaky voice. "We agreed you could lift one curse, witch. And one curse has been lifted, so close down this workshop now or my curse-hatched crows will close down your farm. We'll steal your seed, poison your water and blight your land, just as we promised."

Atacama whispered, "He smells like a crow. I think I've seen him... around. Is he a shapeshifter?"

No one answered. They were all listening to Mrs Sharpe.

"No, Corbie. You promised that I could hold one more workshop and I could lift one more curse if I promised to stop lifting curses forever after. And I, personally, have not yet lifted a curse this week."

"Then why does one of my curse-hatched lie dead on the field of your old farm? Why is that serpent snaking

through the hills? That curse was lifted as a direct result of your workshop, so that is the one curse we gave you as a concession."

"*I* did not lift it. *I* have not left my farm all night."

"But your pupils lifted it."

"My pupils, not me. Anyway, you and I agreed that the Wyrm of Cut Rigg was the most suitable local curse to set as a task, because the pupils would probably find it too dangerous and difficult."

"Apparently these cursed children are not put off by danger or difficulties."

Mrs Sharpe shrugged. "How could we possibly have known that? You also informed me that if they did look likely to lift the curse, your army of curse-hatched crows could stop them. But your crows failed and my pupils succeeded. So the wyrm is free and the crow is dead. That wyrm will probably annoy someone else soon, then someone else will curse it, another crow will hatch out of your precious stone eggs with a wyrm on its wing and you will have your numbers again.

"But that curse was *not* my one curse. By our agreement, signed in blood, I have the right to lift one curse from one of the pupils attending my workshop. So I will do that. Then I will stop running curse-lifting workshops and your crows will stop flying over my land. That was our agreement. And if you don't honour our agreement, we both know who will force you to keep your promise."

The tall man stood silently for a moment, a breeze sliding over his short glossy black hair and ruffling the feathery fringes on his sleeves. Then he nodded. "One more curse. That's it. But if you lift more than one curse, my winged army will destroy all your fertile land, so you can never raise another crop. That's a promise, and we both know the Keeper prefers dark promises like curses to light fluffy promises like your guarantee to lift them."

He raised his arms, the breeze lifted the tattered fringes on his coat, he shifted into a large black crow and flapped away.

Molly and the other four stepped back from the corner, and crowded together against the wall.

"One curse?" said Innes. "One curse! Did you all hear that?"

"But she guaranteed results..." whispered Molly.

"We need to read the small print," said Atacama.

"We need to *burn* the small print," muttered Innes.

"We need to discuss this calmly," said Beth.

"There's nothing to discuss." Innes took a step away from the rest of them.

"Quiet!" murmured Atacama. "We should talk indoors."

They walked across the farmyard and shoved the red door open. As they stepped into the cold classroom, Molly asked Atacama, "If he smelt like a crow, do I smell like a hare?"

The sphinx smiled. "A little. But it's a nice smell."

Beth closed the door behind them. "What are the curse-hatched? Were the crows that attacked us hatched out by curses?"

Atacama said, "I've never heard of the curse-hatched, but I have seen that man Corbie with small flocks of crows, at the... em... around town. But on the basis of what we just heard, I would speculate—"

"No speculating. Facts only," snapped Innes. "And the fact is we all heard the witch say she would only lift one curse at the end of this workshop."

Innes looked at each of his companions in turn, staring into their eyes. His own expression was hard and angry. "There are five of us, with five curses. All threatening our lives or our essential beings."

"We can't say that, Innes," said Atacama, reasonably. "We still don't know what the toad's curse is—"

"We have *five* curses between us," Innes yelled. "And that lying witch is only going to lift *one*!"

The red door slammed wide open.

"What lying witch?" asked Mrs Sharpe, as she strode in. "I've not been lying to you. Though if you will eavesdrop, you might hear unpleasant things, and if you want to get away with eavesdropping, you should hide your footprints and pawprints better and share your horrified questions more quietly. So. Sit down."

No one moved.

"Sit down, all of you!"

Beth and Molly sat down next to each other and the

toad squatted on the desk beside them. Atacama sat on the floor, dignified as always. But Innes didn't sit down. He leant his weight on a desk at the front, still almost standing, staring right into the witch's face.

Mrs Sharpe nodded. "Well done for last night's task. I've felt bad about that wyrm for years. I'm sorry your reward for success was hearing my argument with Corbie. But you had to find out sometime."

She took a deep breath and said calmly, "I will, indeed, only lift one curse at the end of this workshop."

"One curse? Just one curse?" said Innes, in a slow cold voice. "What about your guarantee?"

"My guarantee is quite clear. And you don't need to read the small print, Atacama, it's on the flyer, in public view."

She pulled a flyer from her cardigan and read, "Guaranteed result." She held it out. "See? 'Result.' Singular. Not plural. One result. One curse lifted. It's right there, in black and red."

"But every other year, you've lifted everyone's curses," whispered Beth.

"Yes, but this year my farm is under threat from a huge flock of crows. Curse-hatched crows need the energy of curses to survive. Every new curse hatches out one more crow, and that crow lives for as long as the curse lasts. Recently the leader of the curse-hatched crows, Corbie, realised that if he prevents curses being lifted, he can increase their numbers and strength.

"Corbie decided to threaten my farm, to force me to

stop running my curse-lifting workshops. I must protect my land, because my power grows from the fertility of my earth. Therefore I agreed to stop running these workshops, because I couldn't run them anyway without the power of my land to back them up, but I bargained for one more year and one more curse. So I will lift one curse. I wonder whose curse it will be?"

She looked round them all. They glanced suspiciously at each other.

Molly asked, "How will you decide?"

"One last task, of course. The first to complete it will get their curse lifted."

"So, tell us, witch," said Innes. "What is the last task?"

Mrs Sharpe pulled a roll of parchment from the cupboard and laid it on the desk. It unfurled, revealing several different sheets rolled up together.

"The last task is to steal a stone egg from those curse-hatched crows, then do a good deed with it and bring it to me. The first to arrive here carrying a stone egg charged with goodness rather than darkness will have their curse lifted, as promised. And the rest of you… I'm sorry I can't do more, but perhaps you've learnt something useful from your days on my farm."

"We've learnt never to trust a witch," said Beth.

Mrs Sharpe pointed at the creamy sheets on the desk. "Here are five maps showing the location of the stone eggs, because perhaps you won't want to share one map. The maps will last until Friday, then the ink will fade away.

There will always be food and shelter in the bunkhouse. And I won't even expect you to dig more fields, so you can concentrate on this task." She looked up again. "I hope to see at least one of you back here before the end of the week."

Mrs Sharpe turned and walked out, closing the door gently behind her.

Innes reached forward and picked up a map. He turned round and looked at them all. "Don't get in my way." Then he walked out.

Beth stood up, collected a map and said, "Thanks for saving my life, Molly. I will return the favour. But not this week." And she left.

Atacama used his claws to pull down a map. He studied it, then pushed it away. He looked up at Molly, still sitting at the desk. "The rest of us understand magical dangers better than you do. Perhaps you should accept your curse, rather than compete with us for this egg." He left too.

Molly was alone with the toad.

"I don't think we're a team any more," she said.

The toad jumped down and walked slowly out of the classroom.

Molly sat on her own, thinking about the sphinx's advice. Then she stood, picked up a map and went to search for a stone egg.

Chapter Eighteen

Molly had learned how to read a map on an orienteering project in Primary 6, but the witch's map didn't look like any map she'd seen before. As well as the usual rivers, roads and contour lines, it had unfamiliar symbols in gold and silver, and curly lettered warnings about the homes of local brownies and basilisks.

It appeared to be a map of magical locations around Craigvenie. Mrs Sharpe's farm was in the centre, and in the bottom left corner was a shimmering golden arrow pointing to the words: *Stone Egg Wood* and a tiny picture of an arch. So that's where Molly had to go.

But how could she get there? She looked closer at the map. There was a road leading out of Craigvenie that would take her two thirds of the way. Then she'd have to go cross-country.

She didn't have time to study the map properly. Both Innes and Atacama were incredibly fast, and would get to the Stone Egg Wood long before her. Beth was quicker on a bike than she was. Molly had no idea what the toad's powers were, apart from supernaturally efficient toilet-building, but it would probably beat her to the wood too.

Molly knew it was unlikely she would complete this task before any of her former teammates, but she wasn't going to give up. Not without a race.

She ran to the shed, planning to cycle part of the way. The bikes she and Beth had ridden to Cut Rigg Farm were still leaning against the wall. Did Beth have a faster form of transport?

Then Molly noticed that all four tyres had been slashed. The wheel rims of both bikes were resting on the ground. She couldn't tell whether the cuts were made by a knife, a claw or teeth. But it didn't really matter.

The slashes made it absolutely clear that the five of them were no longer helping each other.

They weren't even racing each other.

Now they were sabotaging each other.

So Molly started walking.

She headed briskly down the lane, trying to read the map as she strode along, looking at the odd symbols and notations on either side of the route to Stone Egg Wood.

Devil's Cauldron
Giant's Cradle
Wolf Stane

Molly would probably try to avoid those locations.

She remembered, with a faint reluctant ache in her muscles, that when her teacher had taken them orienteering, they *ran* between control points. It wouldn't be as fast as cycling, but she should give it a go.

After tracing her fingers along the route to double check she was heading southwest towards the mountains, she folded the map, put it in her back pocket and started to jog.

In the first ten minutes, Molly was overtaken by a library van, a whisky lorry and a family out for a day-trip on their bikes, including a giggling four year old on a glittery bike.

Molly sighed. She was already losing this race. Not just to the irregular traffic on the narrow road, she was losing to the white horse, the black sphinx and probably the dryad and toad as well. Unless she could find a faster way to travel, she would fail at this task before she even began.

As she ran towards higher ground, her legs started to feel heavy. She couldn't keep up this pace for much longer.

She couldn't run all the way. Not as a girl.

But she could run all the way as a hare. And much faster.

She stopped and leant forward, hands on knees, gasping for breath.

Did she want to become a hare? Even if she did want to, how could she shift without a dog's bark to trigger the curse?

Molly looked at the fields by the road. She looked at the bare earth and soft grass, and she knew how it would feel to run on that ground as a hare. She would feel light

and free. She would feel capable of winning any race and completing any task.

But could she deliberately choose to be a hare? Should she?

She clambered off the road, over the verge and fence, into the field. And she said, "Woof."

Nothing happened. Obviously. She sounded like a child reading a picture book about doggies. Dogs didn't say 'woof' any more than ducks said 'quack' or mice said 'squeak'.

She thought about the dogs that had barked at her this week, the dogs that had triggered her change.

Molly licked her lips and yipped like the small dog by the river.

She looked at her hands, which were still hands.

Then she tensed her stomach muscles and tried a deep bark like Mr Crottel's wolfhound.

Her hands were still pale human skin.

In her frustration, with no words to express how she felt about this ridiculous desire to be a hare, Molly growled, like one of Atacama's purrs, vibrating at the back of her throat. As she growled, she felt a brief ripple of warmth up her spine.

She thought, dogs don't just bark. They also growl.

She closed her eyes and thought about how frustrated she was that she couldn't run faster as a girl, and also how frustrated those dogs were when they couldn't catch her as a hare.

She imagined herself running from a dog, bouncing, leaping, flying through the air. She imagined how the dog felt, watching its prey get away.

And from that frustration, she growled, deep in her throat.

Gurrrrrr.

Suddenly she felt a flash of welcome heat up and down her spine.

She opened her eyes and looked down at the earth, just below her nose. And at her own brown paws.

I hope I don't regret this, she thought. I hope I can change back.

But she didn't regret it. Not for one second. She bounced and she leapt and she ran. Not dodging, not zigzagging, not trying to escape. She wasn't trying to escape from a predator, and she wasn't trying to escape from herself either.

She ran like she'd seen Innes run. In a straight line, aiming for a goal and powering towards it. She ran towards the wild lands of the Cairngorms, towards Stone Egg Wood.

Then, as she leapt over a low wall, she was falling, rolling over herself, banging knees and elbows.

She shook her head. She'd crossed a boundary into someone else's land. So, just like falling off a bike, she had to get right back on.

She growled again, a deep wild sound, to call the wild animal inside her. And the hare came back.

So Molly ran and leapt and stretched into her fastest speed.

The next time she shifted back to a girl, she put her hand in her back pocket. She grinned. Just as her clothes reappeared when she became human, so did the hair bobble, the twenty-pence piece and the folded map in her pocket.

She growled and ran again.

Molly followed the line of the road, running through the fields and, when the land became too high and scrubby for crops, running across wild grass and heather.

Then the road curved round a hill and she crashed to the ground again as a girl. She checked the map. It was time to leave the guidance of the road and set off cross-country. She took her bearings from the high mountains in the distance, growled, and ran into the moors towards the Stone Egg Wood.

Molly couldn't see trees or walls or anything ahead that looked like a magical wood. But she knew she was running in the right direction. She had to trust the map.

So she ran and ran.

She suspected that this wasn't how hares were meant to run. They sprinted when they were chased, they didn't run for hours and hours. However, she had a girl's mind and determination inside this hare's body, and she'd keep her fast legs running for as long as necessary.

Anyway, her hare legs weren't getting tired the way her human legs had on the road. Maybe she had endless hare energy for running, like Innes had endless kelpie energy for work.

She didn't know who owned this bare land. Whoever it was, they owned a great big chunk of it, because she hadn't stumbled over into her girl self since she left the road.

Which was a problem. If she couldn't shift back to a girl, how could she read the map, and how could she find and steal and carry a stone egg?

Molly stopped and crouched on the fragrant damp ground.

There was no point continuing to run, even though she wasn't tired. She had to check the map or she might run past the entrance.

She had turned herself into a hare. Could she turn herself back?

Molly thought about being a girl. About her hands and fingers, her feet and toes, her freckled skin.

But she stayed a hare.

She thought about stumbling and falling when she crossed a boundary. About ripped jeans and clumsy limbs.

But she stayed a hare.

She tried to say her name, but her mouth couldn't form the words.

And she stayed a hare.

So, she could manipulate the curse to shift into a hare, but she couldn't shift back without a boundary.

She stood on her hind legs, stretched as high as she could and looked around for anything that might mark a

change of land ownership: a wall, a fence, a track.

But there was nothing. Just dark bumpy land, bright glimmers of water and white windmills dancing in the distance.

Then she realised there was one long unbroken glimmer of water to the southwest. Not a pool or a marsh. A narrow river.

That might be a boundary.

She sprinted towards the river, then leapt across. She landed hard, just before the opposite bank, soaking her clothes, and bashing her shoulder on the slimy stones.

She was a girl again.

She clambered out, dripping and bruised, but taller, with useful hands.

Molly stood on the riverbank and scanned the landscape. There was no wood, no big group of trees, for miles. The only trees were stunted windblown birches, most of them shorter than her, growing in the occasional shelter where the river cut through low rises of earth.

Then she noticed a purple-and-black shape by one of the largest, most crooked birches. A bike.

Molly ran over. It was a mountain bike, chunky and muddy. This must be Beth's own bike.

So the bad news was that Beth had already arrived, but the good news was that the entrance must be nearby.

Molly pulled out the map and sat down to study it.

By the words *Stone Egg Wood,* there was a tiny sketch of a low dark arch.

An arch in a wall? But there were no walls around here.

An arch in a cliff? But the mountains were miles to the south, and they were lumpy heathery slopes, not slabs of rock.

An arch in what?

This land wasn't really flat, it was bumpy, with slices cut through the bumps by water, by peat cutters, by sheep and deer tracks. Perhaps there was a low dark arch in one of these peaty banks?

The dryad would have left her bike by the tree nearest the arch. Molly stood beside the bike and looked carefully around her.

She suddenly saw a black patch on a nearby slope of brown peaty earth. She walked over. It was an archway, carved into the ground. The same low curved shape as the arch on the map.

So Molly took a deep breath and stepped into the hole in the dark earth.

Chapter Nineteen

The tunnel was damp, peaty smelling, and slightly warmer than the air outside. It became darker as Molly moved further from the sunlight, round gentle downward bends. But after a few moments blundering forward, she saw a blur of dim blue-ish light ahead.

As she got closer, she saw the light was coming through an open door, one of a pair of white wooden doors across the width of the tunnel. The two doors were covered in carved trees with birds and nests balanced in their branches and with snakes, people, horses and flames writhing around their roots.

Then Molly noticed words carved on ribbons round the trunks of the trees. When she followed the ribbons across from the open door to the closed door, the words read:

Welcome.
This door welcomes our friends.
If you are a friend, whisper your name to the carving of the bird who invited you, and the door will let you in.

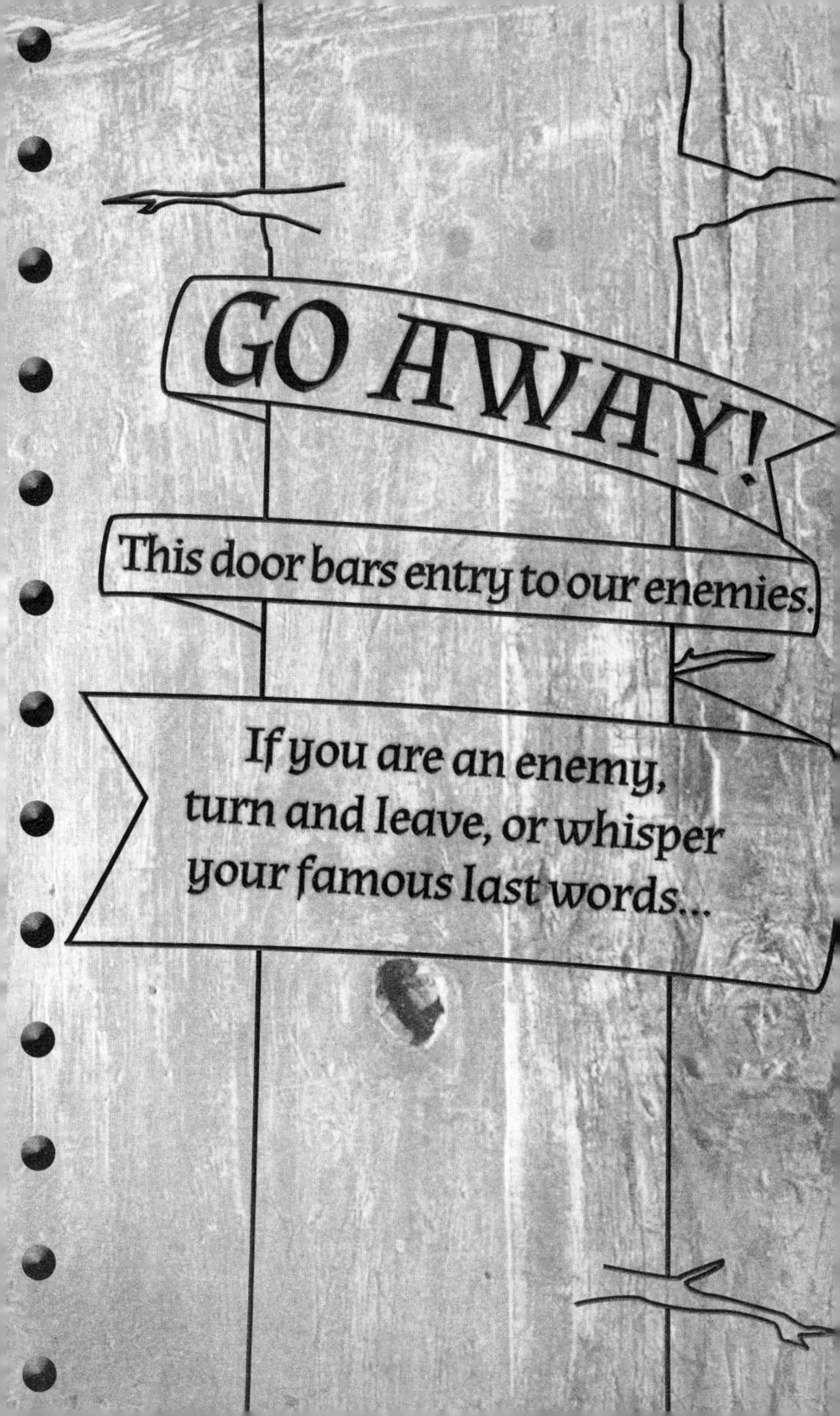
GO AWAY!
This door bars entry to our enemies.
If you are an enemy,
turn and leave, or whisper
your famous last words...

Molly frowned. Who had opened the door? Had one of her former teammates whispered the right name to the right carved bird? Molly didn't have to work it out though, because the door was still open.

So she stepped cautiously through into Stone Egg Wood.

She found herself in a long hall, dimly lit by glowing blue mosses on the floor, filled with trees reaching upwards to the almost impossibly high roof, where warm yellow light poured in through open slits.

The trees were leafless and barkless. She touched the nearest stripped trunk. It was cold and felt more like stone than wood.

She looked around. All the trees were pale grey, mineral-coloured, glittering like mica. Was this a wood of stone trees, as well as stone eggs?

She walked further into the hall, moving quietly on the glowing moss, glancing back every few steps to make sure she didn't lose sight of the door.

Who else was here? Who had opened that door? Where were the eggs?

Ahead of her, Molly saw a wide open space and a glint of water beyond. The curse-hatched crows had found or created a complete cold hard landscape, hidden under the moor.

She looked up and saw nests woven from white twigs and blue gems, held high in the stone trees' branches, far out of reach.

The stone eggs must be in those nests, thought Molly.

And higher than the nests, she saw birds. Hundreds of roosting black crows, silent and still, sleeping in the topmost twigs.

Then Molly saw movement to her right.

She hid behind a trunk and watched a black shape trying to climb a tree. Atacama, slipping down faster than he could climb up.

She heard a familiar laugh and a whisper. "Your claws are no good on stone." Innes was also trying to climb a tree, also slipping down.

Molly shook her head. If they gave each other a leg up, one of them could probably reach the lowest branches. But they weren't helping each other; they were trying to climb different trees.

She didn't want them to know she was here. She moved to her left, hoping to find an easier tree.

Instead, she found Beth.

She nearly stood on the dryad, who was slumped at the base of a slim stone trunk.

Beth was gasping, struggling for breath.

Molly knelt down and touched the dryad's white cheek. Beth was freezing cold. Her green eyes opened and she whispered, "Molly! I can't move..."

Molly touched the glowing moss with her fingertips. It was warm. The air was warm. "Why are you so cold?"

"The trees... are fossilised. The trees... are stone. I'm turning to..." She gasped again. "Must get out, but can't move..."

Molly grabbed Beth's hand. Her fingers were stiff and unbending.

"Obviously I *could* save your life again," whispered Molly, "but I didn't think we were doing that this week. I could come back next week..."

Beth moaned softly and closed her eyes.

Molly sighed. "Of course I'll help. It's not like I'm throwing away a realistic chance to win this task. Come on." She slid her arms under Beth's oxters and dragged the dryad as quietly as she could towards the doors.

Not quietly enough. The sleeping birds didn't hear her, but the kelpie did.

Molly looked up to find Innes standing between her and the open door.

"What are you doing, hare-girl?"

"She's turning to stone. I'm getting her out of here."

"You don't have to do that. It's everyone for themselves now. You've no chance of beating me anyway, but you'll certainly never win if you stop to help your rivals."

"I know. But I couldn't leave her here."

The kelpie was staring at her, frowning at her.

"Innes, I couldn't just step over her."

"Why not?" he said. "I did."

He walked towards another tree and tried to reach his arms around the smooth trunk.

Molly dragged Beth out the open doorway. It wasn't easy pulling her along the soft peaty tunnel, but as they

got further from the stone trees she warmed up and began to push with her feet.

When they reached the open air, Molly hoisted Beth upright and helped her to the river. The dryad slumped on the bank, splashed her face in the water and said, "Thank you. Again."

"It's ok. I'd better get back in."

"No, wait," said Beth. "How did you get here?"

"How did *you* get here? Did you cycle all the way?"

"Just the last bit. Uncle Pete gave me a lift most of the way in his Land Rover. How did you get here so fast?"

"I'm a part-time hare, remember. I'd better go back."

"Wait. Has Innes stolen his egg yet?"

"No, he's still trying to climb up a tree. Did he get in first? How did you all get through that door?"

"Innes opened the door just before I arrived. He didn't kick it in; that would have been too noisy. I assume he worked out the password. I heard him telling Atacama that he'd have closed the door and shut the rest of us in the tunnel, but he needed to leave himself a clear exit. I'm sure Innes will get up a tree eventually. He's quite determined."

"Determined is one word for him," said Molly. "Also selfish, ruthless, hard-hearted..."

Beth sighed. "I can't win the task now, without an egg. I didn't realise the trees would be so cold and dangerous, and no one expected them to be so difficult to climb." Then she smiled, very slightly. "It would be nice if someone could beat Innes. How was Atacama doing?"

"Like a cat trying to run up a glass door. Not dignified and not getting to the top."

"Are you any good at climbing trees, Molly?"

"Not stone ones."

"Not even with a rope?"

Molly smiled. "A rope would help. Do you have one?"

"I brought the bark rope I made at Cut Rigg Farm, just in case. It's in the pannier of my bike. Take it, if you like."

Molly walked over to the bike, opened the bag and pulled out the coil of thin brown rope.

"It's strong, it will hold your weight. Good luck."

Molly nodded to Beth and ran back into the tunnel, which didn't seem as dark or as long now she knew how close the door was and what she would find beyond it.

She saw Innes and Atacama, still slipping down the smooth trunks, still failing to climb them.

She searched for a tree of her own, nowhere near the sphinx or the kelpie, with nests on the lowest branches.

Soon she found one with a short spiky branch about two metres above her head. There were a couple of nests balancing in forks of a thick branch just a little higher up.

Molly tied a loop at the end of the rope, whirled it like a lasso and threw it up towards the spiky branch.

It missed and fell onto her face.

She tried again.

It landed over the branch, but slid right off.

Molly took a step back for a better angle and threw one more time.

The rope fell over the branch and stayed there. Molly tugged and it held firm.

She hadn't thought to tie knots in the rope before she threw it, and she'd never mastered gripping a rope with her feet to climb up, so she just hauled herself upwards, her hands pulling on the rope and her feet walking awkwardly up the tree trunk.

After a bit of inelegant scrambling, she was sitting astride the thick forked branch. She glanced at the dozen crows perched above her, but they were fast asleep in the topmost branches.

So she shuffled along and looked into the nearest white nest.

It was filled with eggs. Seven eggs. All smooth and shiny. All different muted colours: cream, grey, pale blue, green… Some spotted, some plain, some faintly striped. All the same size, just a little smaller than hen's eggs.

She reached out and touched a pale green egg with chocolate-brown speckles.

The egg was made of stone. Cold, hard, slippy, polished. She tapped a fingernail against it. Tip tap. It didn't sound hollow. Then a tiny answering tap came back. Tip tap. She jerked her hand away.

She heard another sound close by. A soft peeping squeak. She leant over to look in the other nest, further along the branch.

In the middle of the nest, surrounded by a yellow jigsaw of broken eggshell, was a baby bird.

The tiny bird, with knobbly pink wings and huge dark eyes, looked up at her. It was almost naked, with just a few faint pencil lines of skinny dark feathers.

The chick opened its beak wide, the bright orange mouth seeming bigger than its head. As it wobbled towards her, asking for food, it stretched out its short wings. On one wing, Molly could see a clear image.

A hare.

A long-legged brown hare, leaping across the pink skin of the bird's wing.

She remembered the wyrm on the wing of the dead crow at Cut Rigg Farm. This must be the crow linked to her curse. The baby crow that had hatched out of a stone egg the moment she was cursed.

This was her own curse-hatched.

This baby bird, gazing up at her, opening its beak and jerking its wings, was connected to the curse that could kill her the next time she was chased by a fast dog or ran across a busy road.

Molly wondered whether the curse would break if the curse-hatched was killed. She stared at the baby bird, who was gazing back up at her, peeping quietly. And she realised she wasn't prepared to harm this chick to find out.

The serpent had escaped its curse while the curse-hatched crow was still alive. The bird fell from the sky when the curse was lifted. Presumably the curse kept the crow alive, not the other way round.

If she lifted her curse, would this baby bird die?

She looked at the red marks on her hands where she had been pecked by crows last night. This little pink nestling would grow into a vicious crow, ready to hurt and kill to keep its curse alive.

But right now, as it cheeped at her, she reached her hand out and touched its naked head. The chick pushed warmly against her hand and opened its beak again. It wanted her to feed it.

"I don't have any worms for you, sorry."

Then she heard a scraping noise below. Molly lifted her hand away from the nest and looked down.

She saw Innes climbing fast and efficiently up the bark rope towards her.

Molly wondered if she could unhook the rope, so the kelpie would fall. But if she couldn't hurt a baby bird that carried her curse, she certainly couldn't injure a boy who'd nearly become her friend.

She couldn't let him take all the stone eggs though. She needed one for herself.

She shoved her hand into the nearest nest. Her fingers wrapped round two eggs. She glanced at them – one pale biscuit brown, one lilac – then slipped them both into her fleece pocket and zipped it up.

Innes pulled himself onto the branch.

He was shaking his head. "Oh dear, Molly. You're not ruthless enough to win this task. You should have pulled the rope up after you so no one could follow. Or you should have loosened it once I started climbing. But you didn't. So, get out of my way, while I find my egg."

Molly didn't move.

Innes shifted along the branch, closer to her. "Let me past and no one needs to get hurt."

She looked at his face. He wasn't smiling at her, but he didn't look angry either. He just looked determined.

She'd hesitated about dropping Innes to the ground, but she was sure he wouldn't hesitate to push her off if she didn't give him what he wanted.

"There are enough eggs for all of us," she said calmly and leant out of the way, so he could stretch past her.

"Thanks for being sensible," he said, as he chose a watery-blue egg. Then he saw the other nest and leant further over. "A baby curse-hatched! Someone's curse is feeding that chick."

"Mine," whispered Molly. "It's my curse. There's a hare on its wing."

"Really?" He looked at her and frowned, then he looked at the bird again. "I wonder what would happen if..."

"No!" she said quickly. "I don't want to try that. I think the crow needs the curse, but I don't think the curse needs the crow."

"You're probably right. But if I find the crow that carries my father's curse, I will wring its neck. Just to see what happens."

Then he smiled. "So, I have the first egg!" He slid off the branch and jumped to the ground, bending his knees for a steady landing.

He looked up. "I've very kindly left you the rope, so you can get down safely. But don't try to catch up with me, Molly. And keep your hood up and your head down for the next few minutes, it's about to get nasty in here." He grinned and ran towards the door.

Molly half-jumped, half-slid down the rope, and as she crash-landed on the moss, she noticed Atacama trying a new tactic. The sphinx was clawing his way up a soft peaty wall, then once he was high enough, he was swiping at nests in the nearest trees.

As he swiped and slid and fell onto his paws, a nest fell down with him. Molly nodded. Now Atacama had an egg too.

Then she heard a shout. The first loud noise in the hall since she'd arrived.

Innes was standing by the white double doors. "EGG THIEVES!" he yelled. "Someone is stealing your eggs!"

Then the kelpie ran out, slamming the open door behind him.

Molly heard a sleepy cawing and flapping above her. The crows were waking up.

Chapter Twenty

Molly heard the echo of the slam as she sprinted towards the door. When she reached it, there was no handle to pull and no carving to persuade.

She flinched away from a black shape suddenly appearing at her side. But it wasn't a crow. It was Atacama, his normally sleek fur filthy with peat, carrying a pearly grey egg in his mouth.

"I can't believe Innes shut us in," Molly muttered.

Atacama placed the egg on the ground. "Can't you? Then you don't know him very well."

Molly looked up. She saw the crows, clacking their beaks, shaking their wings open, flapping groggily upwards, gathering and circling in the high roof-space.

"How can we get out?" she whispered. "They'll notice us any minute."

"The door isn't completely shut. Look..." The sphinx pointed at a hairline crack between the two white doors. "That vicious little kelpie slammed it so hard, it bounced back a little. I'll try to hook my claw in there to pull it open, if you stand sentry."

Molly looked up. The crows were circling in greater and greater numbers, shrieking at each other like they were planning an assault.

She glanced down again. Atacama was lying on the moss, stretching his paw out, trying to fit his claw into the crack without pushing the door completely shut.

She was meant to be the sentry, so she looked up again. Straight into the eyes of a crow on a branch in the nearest tree.

The crow opened its beak.

"Atacama, they've spotted us!"

As the crow screeched and swooped towards Molly, she looked down to see Atacama knocking his egg through the gap he'd opened, then sliding sinuously through himself.

Molly slid after him.

Once they were both in the tunnel, the sphinx said, "We should leave the door open, in case Beth or the toad are still inside."

Before Molly could say that Beth was already out safely, he'd picked up his egg and sprinted away.

Molly heard cawing behind the door and considered slamming it shut, but she didn't know where the toad was, so she left it ajar and ran up the tunnel.

When she saw the arch of light ahead she screamed, "Beth, if you're still there, hide! The crows are awake!"

She fell out into the daylight, just in time to watch:

A white horse galloping north far in the distance;

A black cat running after him;

A purple-haired dryad stepping between two crooked birch trees and vanishing.

Molly turned round to see crows billowing out of the high ground above the archway, from every hidden split and gap in the fragile peaty land. Crows rising out of the earth in sudden sharp lines of black.

Molly growled, shifted, then slipped into the nearest dip in the ground and crouched down. She lay there, ears flat to her back, paws tucked in.

Hidden and still.

She could hear the crows shrieking above her.

More birds flew out of the earth, diving up into the sky to join the circling rings of crows, calling and screaming. Then a line of crows peeled off and chased after the sphinx and the horse. The remaining crows flew down to search the land, the river, the trees.

But Molly stayed still.

Her girl self wanted to run, but her hare self knew that if she stayed still she would blend into the earth.

In the chaos of noise and feathers, Molly kept her nerve and kept still.

Without moving her head, she could see the birch trees to her left. She was sure that the tree nearer the water was taller and straighter since Beth stepped between them. Was Beth *inside* that tree?

The crows swooped in lines and gangs and swirls.

Crows skimmed up and down the river. Crows dived between the two trees. Crows flew in and out of the tunnel mouth.

But they didn't see Molly on the ground and they couldn't find Beth among the trees. So after five minutes of searching and screaming, they circled high above once more, then went suddenly silent.

Molly felt a moment of skin-tingling fear. Had they noticed her? Was that the signal to attack?

Then she saw the crows flying off in a black arrow, following the smaller group that was chasing Innes and Atacama.

As the black birds became indistinct in the distance, Molly stood squarely on all four paws, stretched her long legs and arched her back. Then she ran at the river and leapt over it.

She landed in the middle of the water, soaking her jeans again.

She stood up and turned round, to see Beth step out from between the trees, both of which were low and crooked again.

Molly clambered back onto the bank. "Did you hide in the tree?"

Beth nodded. "It was a bit cramped."

The dryad sat by the river, looking warmer and stronger than when Molly had dragged her from the tunnel. Molly sat down beside her.

Beth asked, "Did you find an egg?"

Molly unzipped her pocket and checked inside. She nodded.

Beth almost smiled. "Good for you. You have as much chance as anyone else now. Speed and aggression won't help Innes or Atacama with a good deed. They'll have to slow down and think." The dryad sighed. "I'd better go home and tell my family I've failed."

Molly pulled her hand out of her pocket. "You haven't failed. Not yet. I didn't get one stone egg. I got two. You can have one."

Beth gasped. "Why would you give me an egg? We're meant to be rivals. Only one of us can complete Mrs Sharpe's task and get our curse lifted."

"I know, but I think you should have the same chance as the rest of us."

Molly looked at the two eggs. A biscuity brown one with coppery glints, and a lilac one with silver veins. She gave Beth the purple egg.

Beth held it gently in her hand, stroked it and smiled at Molly. "Thank you very much. I hope you don't regret it."

Molly smiled. "I won't. Good luck."

"Good luck to you too." Beth stood up and walked over to her bike. "You were a hare when I was hiding. How did you transform without a dog scaring you?"

Molly shrugged, and waded over the river. "Maybe you were right about Mr Crottel not being a powerful magic user. The curse is quite easy to fool. It's not about the dog scaring me, it's about the noise the dog makes. See..."

She growled, and in one hot heartbeat she was a hare, all four paws braced to run.

Beth frowned. "You're trying to lift your curse, Molly, not learn to live with it." She wheeled her bike through the shallow water, then pedalled away over the uneven ground.

Molly overtook Beth easily, but she knew the dryad was right: speed alone wasn't enough to complete the task first.

Mrs Sharpe's map showed the homes of local magical beings, so perhaps Molly could find someone nearby who needed help. The next time she crossed a boundary and became a girl, she'd examine the map for an opportunity to do her good deed fast enough to win the task and have her curse lifted by the witch.

Chapter Twenty-One

Giant's Chair
Dragon's Knowe
Troll Moss

Molly frowned at the map. None of the beings with homes marked nearby seemed likely to need help from an eleven-year-old girl and a small smooth stone egg.

Now that she sat by the narrow road and thought about it, why would *anyone* need a good deed done with a stone egg? What are stone eggs good for?

She looked up and saw a few heavy clouds to the south, blurring the glow of the sun, but not hiding the sharp pale daytime moon just above the horizon. She looked down at her soggy trainers and damp jeans. She'd like to get her good deed done and her curse lifted before that rain got here and soaked the rest of her.

But what could she use a stone egg for? Molly's first few thoughts – paperweight, doorstop, blocking a hole – all involved leaving the egg behind. But she needed to give the egg to Mrs Sharpe. So she had to find someone in need of help, who could be helped by a stone egg, and who would let her take the egg away afterwards.

She looked at the map again. Giants and dragons and trolls. She also wanted to find someone who wouldn't eat her or grill her or squash her. Were there any small safe creatures on the map? She peered more closely.

She saw a dot just past Craigvenie marked:

Gorse Village (Flower Fairy dwellings).

Fairies were little, and Molly assumed they were harmless. Then she remembered the fairy who'd cursed Innes's family and realised that even small cute magical beings could be dangerous. Anyway, she didn't want to go all the way past town. That would take too long. She wanted to find someone to help on the way back to Skene Mains.

So she ran her finger down the silver-inked road towards Craigvenie and looked at the symbols either side of it.

As well as magical beings' homes, Mrs Sharpe had marked locations for collecting herbs. Close to where Molly sat was a green triangle marked *Splendid nettle patch.*

Molly decided it was worth a brief detour. She left the roadside and found the nettle patch easily, in the corner of a sheep field. The nettles were tall, leafy and a healthy deep green, vivid in the golden autumn landscape. For people who liked nettles, this probably was a splendid nettle patch.

But Molly didn't see any little houses, nor a queue of tiny creatures with placards saying:

I NEED
HELP FROM
A
STONE EGG!

She did notice something pale on the ground. A curved stone, like a shallow bowl, with faint green stains on it. Molly was reminded of the mortar and pestle for grinding ingredients, which were kept on a high shelf in Aunt Doreen's kitchen. She pulled the stone egg from her pocket and placed it in the stone bowl. It could work for grinding spices, herbs or even nettles.

Then she heard a faint sing-song voice.

"Ninety-four leaves, ninety-five leaves, ninety-six leaves..."

Someone was in the nettles! Molly stepped back and looked around. Against the grey stone wall, she saw a neat pile of leaves: all big and juicy and jagged-edged. Someone was harvesting nettles.

The voice sang, "A hundred leaves!"

A little woman, dressed in dusty green, with bright white hair and skin so wrinkled she looked like a forgotten apple, stepped out of the nettle patch.

Molly stared at her and the old woman stared back.

The woman was very short. She didn't even reach Molly's waist. And she was clutching a bundle of leaves to her chest.

Molly wondered who she was looking at. A short human? A slim dwarf? A tall pixie? A well-dressed brownie? Or something that she'd never heard of? The pointed ears and purple eyes were probably clues, but Molly didn't know what they meant, and suspected it would be rude to ask.

So she smiled politely and said, "Can I help you with your nettles? I have a lovely stone egg here, which fits into that mortar. Or maybe that pestle, I'm not sure which bit is which... Would you like those nettles ground? I'd be happy to help."

"Nettles... ground?" muttered the old woman. "Yes, nettles, ground!"

Molly said, "Fantastic! I'll get right on with it then."

She grabbed the nettle leaves beside the wall, ignoring the sting in her fingers, piled them in the shallow bowl-shaped stone and squished them with the stone egg.

She rolled and pressed and crushed, and the nettle leaves mushed down into dark fibres and fragrant juice, staining the bowl and Molly's hands, but leaving the smooth egg unstained.

The little old lady squeaked, "NO! My nettles!" Molly looked up. The little old lady was bouncing up and down. "Ruining my nettles!"

"I thought you wanted your nettles ground." Molly stopped grinding. "I was trying to help."

"I don't want nettles ground. Nettles *from* the ground. Silly girl. Dottled quine. I harvest nettles for clothes. For aprons, skirts, vests and knickers. I can't make knickers with messy squished nettles. Silly daft dottled quine!"

The old lady counted the nettles in her hand. "Twenty leaves. I need a hundred leaves. You pick me eighty more." The old lady, tiny and wrinkled and squeaky and apparently wearing nettle pants, pointed sternly at the nettle patch.

Molly sighed. "Yes. Of course. I'm sorry. I'll pick you more nettles."

With her egg back in her pocket and her fingers stained green, Molly stepped into the nettle patch and picked eighty of the biggest, greenest, stingiest nettle leaves she'd ever touched.

She counted out loud, but she could still hear the little old lady muttering behind her. "Silly quine. Making soup of my nettles rather than knickers. Daftie baftie."

Molly counted, "Seventy-eight, seventy-nine, eighty," then waded out of the deep green stinging sea. "Here you are. Is there anything else, by any chance, that me and my stone egg can do for you? Any good deed?"

"No, silly girl has done too much already." The little old lady sniffed the pile of nettles. She looked up and smiled. "You picked fresh leaves from the tallest nettles. Leaves I can't reach. So I will give you advice in return. Good deeds are hard to do. Interfering is rarely welcome. Better to

wait for someone to ask for help. So keep your ears open. And wash your hands, manky girl."

Molly thanked the old lady for her advice, ran out of sight of the nettle patch, shifted into a hare and bounded down the road, her paws smarting from the nettle stings.

The old lady was right. Finding people who wanted help, then giving them the right help, especially with a stone egg, wasn't going to be easy. Molly decided she would follow the advice and only help people who asked, rather than blunder in with unwanted help.

Perhaps stealing the stone egg had been the simple bit of this task.

Molly was slowing down now, because as she got nearer Craigvenie, boundaries were crashing in more frequently and she kept falling to the ground as a girl.

She crossed a low bridge and tumbled to the ground for the third time in five minutes. As she limped off the bridge, she noticed a clump of docken leaves, so she decided to take a quick break, soothe her stings and look at the map again.

Molly sat down and rubbed both hands with moist docken leaves, easing the pain of the stings. She heard the gentle shushing of water under the bridge. She unfolded the map and saw that this river ran behind Beth's wood. She was getting very near Craigvenie.

Then Molly heard coughing and choking. Perhaps someone needed help!

She followed the sound down a slope, past a field of ponies with broken jumps and a metal horse trough.

Molly slid to a halt on the edge of a deep brown pool and saw a silver fish in the middle of the pool, with its head out of the water. The fish was coughing and spluttering.

"Are you alright? Can I do anything to help?"

The fish swivelled round to look at her and said in a clear musical voice, "I would appreciate some help, thank you."

The fish swam to the bank and spat out a golden ring, big enough to go on a man's thumb and carved with a swirling Celtic design. "I must swallow this ring, so I can give it to the rightful owner when they catch me in nine years' time. But the ring is too big to swallow. Could you...?"

Molly nodded quickly. "I could squash it a little, with this stone egg, if that would help."

Molly picked up the ring, wet with peaty water and fish spit, and looked round for a flat stone.

She saw a mossy boulder a few steps further along the bank, near the ponies' fence. She cleared a small patch of the moss and laid the ring on the bare rock.

"Are you sure you want me to bash this ring? You won't change your mind?"

"I'm sure," said the fish. "You would be doing me a considerable favour."

Molly unzipped her pocket.

A voice said, "Oh no. This is my river, and I'll do any water-based good deeds."

Innes climbed over the fence.

Molly fumbled her stone egg out of her pocket and lifted it up.

Innes strode forward and put his hand between the egg and the ring. "No you don't. I will crush your ring for you, wise old salmon. Step back, Molly Drummond, and no one needs to get hurt."

"No. The last time you said 'no one needs to get hurt' you shut us in with those angry crows. This time I'm not giving into your threats or bullying. The fish asked me to crush the ring, and that's what I'm going to do. So *you* step back, kelpie."

They stood facing each other, the rock between them.

Innes laughed. "I will never step back. But I can make you step back. I can make you RUN, Molly!"

Innes shifted, faster than she'd ever seen, into the horse. Into the form Atacama had said she must fear.

As he shifted, she heard his voice ringing in her ears: 'RUN, Molly!'

But if she ran, she would be running away from her last chance to lift her own curse.

So she didn't run.

"He's a kelpie, child," said the fish. "He's a kelpie, he looks hungry and he's near the water, which is his killing ground. This water is not safe for you, girl. Leave here now."

But Molly shook her head. She wouldn't step back.

She wouldn't run. She wouldn't be bullied by a boy or a horse.

She lifted the egg high above the ring on the rock.

The white horse reared up, hooves cutting the air, and crashed down again, shaking the ground. The rock wobbled and the ring slid off.

Molly glared at him. "Leave me alone, Innes. I'm going to do this..."

The horse bared his long ivory teeth.

And bit her.

The huge heavy horse lunged towards Molly and the kelpie sank his teeth into the shoulder of her fleece, just missing her flesh. He dragged her towards the water.

The fish called out, "Don't let him get you in the water! Give up now and he might let go!"

But it was too late. Molly screamed as the horse lifted her off the ground and galloped into the river, flinging them both into the depths of the pool.

Suddenly Molly was under the water, with cold liquid filling her eyes and mouth and nose.

The pressure on her shoulder lifted. Innes had let go. She tried to swim upwards.

Then she realised she couldn't move, because Innes was still holding her.

But Innes wasn't a horse any more.

Molly could feel tentacles tightening round her legs and torso. She was being pulled deeper into the river, by a kelpie in its monstrous underwater form.

Chapter Twenty-two

The kelpie's tentacles wrapped round Molly's ankles, ribcage and throat, pulling her deeper and deeper into the pool.

She didn't have any air in her lungs. But she wouldn't let Innes drown her so easily.

She jerked her legs and flailed her arms. The ropy tentacles gripped tighter.

She hit out with the stone egg in her fist, hoping to punch some sense into Innes. But she couldn't find a head or a torso, just lots of boneless tentacles. So she smashed at them with the egg and their grip loosened slightly, enough for her to struggle upwards and get her face out of the water to gasp a breath.

But the tentacles tightened again, more and more of them, round her arms and legs and waist, more than she could possibly hope to fight. And the kelpie started to drag her under once more...

Molly took one last look at the sky. At the clouds, the sunlight and the pale daytime sliver of moon. The moon!

Just before she was dragged back under the surface of the water, she screamed, "Innes, the moon! The water isn't safe for you either. Innes, look, the moon!"

Suddenly the tentacles grabbed her much harder, so hard that she realised Innes hadn't been using half his strength before, and he flung her from the water. He threw her up and out, onto the bank.

She collided with the salmon on her way through the water, knocking the fish out of the pool too.

She turned round to see Innes become a boy, a fish, a boy again, then a horse, his shifting fast and unfocussed. The horse scrambled onto the bank beside her.

Molly choked on a sudden harsh salty smell. She whirled round, to see the river turn bright white.

The horse screamed and she saw his back leg was still in the water, salt crystals climbing like upside-down icicles along his hoof.

Innes seemed paralysed with shock, so Molly rolled forward, grabbed his leg and hauled it out of the water, then scrubbed at his hoof to wipe the salt off.

She heard a familiar cough. The salmon, beside her, was drowning in air.

She picked the fish up, to put it back in the river.

"No! Not in there," the salmon croaked, "it's so salty it will poison me."

So she hugged the fish close, scrambled over the fence, ran across the field and dropped it into the dirty water of the horse trough.

"I'll be back with the ring," she gasped. She rushed to the river, wondering if there would still be time to do her good deed.

But Innes was standing by the river, the gold ring flattened and small in his human hand, staring at the water.

The pool was filled with death. With fish and insects and frogs, all floating on the surface, all glittering with salt crystals. All of them dead.

Innes wiped his eyes with a sleeve, then turned to Molly. "Where's the wise salmon?"

"In a horse trough."

"That won't suit his dignity, but thank you for saving his life. And thanks for my life too. The three of us are the only ones to get out of that cursed pool alive. Everything else is dead, and this river will take years to recover."

He sat down and stared at the ring.

"At least you can lift the curse now," said Molly quietly. "You crushed the ring. Give it to the salmon, then take your egg to Mrs Sharpe and get your curse lifted. This won't happen to any more rivers."

Innes closed his fist over the crumpled gold. "I didn't crush the ring just now, while you were saving the fish, after you saved my life. Even I wouldn't do that. The ring was like this when we came out of the water. I must have smashed it with my hoof when I attacked you. So neither of us has done a good deed with an egg yet."

"It's not easy, is it?" said Molly. "I've already failed at a good deed involving nettles."

"Ouch. I've already failed at a good deed involving chickens." He used a handful of grass to clean the remaining salt crystals off his left boot.

Molly sat down beside him. "Innes. Can I ask...? Were you going to drown me? Were you going to eat me?"

Innes shook his head. "I was angry with you. I wanted to frighten you. But I would have let you go, if you'd admitted I had won, if you'd promised to stop interfering."

"I couldn't admit anything or promise anything while I was drowning."

"Obviously. That's why I let you up to get air. So you could surrender. Anyway, my mum says eating friends isn't polite. Or nutritious. Apparently it leaves a bad taste in your mouth. So I probably wouldn't have eaten you, even if you had kept fighting me."

"I'm not going to give up," said Molly.

"I'm starting to realise that. I'm not going to either." He pointed to the creatures floating belly-up in the salty pool. "That's why I can't give up."

Molly said, "I know this curse is life and death for you, but it's the same for each of us."

Innes stood up and offered Molly his hand to pull her up, but she was already half-standing, so she didn't take it. They climbed the fence together and walked to the horse trough. The salmon bobbed up and nodded to them.

Innes said, "Here's your ring, crushed by my hoof rather than a stone egg."

"Thank you, young kelpie. I'm grateful to both of you.

I'd be even more grateful if you could get me out of this cramped horsey water to a clean pool."

Innes glanced at the sky. "It's about to rain, so you'll be fine for a few hours. I'll move you somewhere more spacious once I've lifted the curse that killed your river."

He turned to Molly. "We should split up. Look for different good deeds, not get in each other's way again—"

He was interrupted by a noise. A roaring bellow of pain.

A cry for help.

The noise was coming from Beth's wood.

Molly looked at Innes. "Do you want to see who gets there first, a hare or a horse?"

"I'd love to race you, but we don't have time to find a dog."

Molly smiled. "I don't need to hear a dog any more. Not a real one."

She growled and shifted.

Innes laughed and called out, "Ready, steady, go!"

The horse and the hare raced across the fields towards the woods, the horse leaping over fences, the hare squeezing under them.

Molly ran in a straight line, rather than dodging about. She used her hare's speed, but her human focus. She had to get to the wood to help that screaming creature, and she had to get there before Innes.

At first they kept pace with each other. Two of the

fastest animals in the world, a horse and a hare, both pushing themselves as hard as they could. The hare skimming the ground, the horse thundering above.

The hare was built for running and nothing else. Molly was light and supple, with legs ridiculously long for her body.

But the horse was not built just for running. Innes wasn't a racehorse, all nervy and fragile; he was a strong, heavy horse, able to pull loads and fight in battles as well as gallop.

They leapt over the land, forcing themselves to the fastest pace their bodies could achieve.

And Molly won.

She pulled ahead, inch by inch, pace by pace, leap by leap. She darted into the woods a few heartbeats before Innes did.

Then she tripped and fell to the ground, as a girl.

Molly watched the horse gallop past her into the woods.

There might not be another boundary among the trees, so she couldn't become a hare again. She ran on heavy human legs after the horse, towards the deep roaring noise.

This time, Innes won. He got to the source of the bellowing before Molly.

But he didn't get there first.

When Molly arrived, she saw that Beth, Atacama and the toad were there too.

Beth was jabbing Innes in the chest. "It's my wood, so it's my good deed. Get out of my way." Her pale face was fierce, her purple hair flying around her head in the breeze. "All of you, get out of my wood."

Molly looked past the rivals and saw a white stag trapped in a bramble patch, his antlers tangled and his skin ripped by thorns.

"It's my good deed!" repeated Beth.

"It's the good deed of whoever can free the stag first." Innes shoved the dryad's hand off his chest.

Molly laughed. "If it's about being first, let's race to the stag, Innes. Now we know who's actually faster."

Innes glared at her. "I got here first."

"Only because I crossed a boundary. In this wood, or in a field, or on a racetrack, I'll beat you every time."

Beth said, "It doesn't matter who's faster, it matters who releases the stag." She took a step forward.

Innes grabbed her arm. "No! I *need* this good deed. I have to save my rivers and my life."

Atacama said, "I need my riddle back to be a true sphinx, so I need this good deed too."

The toad opened its mouth, but Molly couldn't hear a croak over the stag's bellowing and her classmates' quarrelling.

Beth said, "But the stag trapped here is a chance to lift this wood's curse. It's *my* good deed!"

Molly took a step back and watched them, yelling and demanding, shoving and pushing. And she felt rain start to fall from the clouds that had been threatening for hours.

"Stop, please!" yelled Molly. "All of you, stop arguing and think! We need to free that stag with calming words and gentle hands. You can't untangle brambles with a

stone egg. How were you planning to use your eggs?"

Beth said, "Bash the thorns off with the egg?"

Atacama said, "Hypnotise the stag to keep it calm, by waving the egg in front of it?"

Innes shrugged. "Knock the stag out with the egg, so it's easier to free it?"

The toad snorted. A comment Molly could hear because the stag was finally quietening down.

Molly said, "I'm leaving my stone egg in my pocket, so I can untangle the stag using both hands. Then I'll search for another good deed, all of my own, without you lot arguing about it."

She shoved Beth and Innes out of the way and walked towards the brambles.

But the stag was already free.

He was standing calmly by the brambles, with Rosalind, Beth's little cousin, grinning beside him. "You were making lots of noise and scaring this poor deer, so I untangled him myself."

She held up her hands. Her left palm was bleeding slightly. "Now I need a plaster."

The stag nudged her with his nose.

Rosalind giggled. "Would you take me home, dear Mister Deer, so I can get a plaster from Auntie Jean? She could put plasters on your cuts too. We have plasters with kittens and plasters with space aliens."

Innes sighed. "Doing good deeds is harder than I expected."

Beth lifted Rosalind up onto the stag's back. "I know. I've made a mess of one with a newt and one with a lark already."

Atacama said, "In the old stories, heroes meet ancient crones or trapped animals in the first dozen steps of their journey, do good deeds for them, then get favours in return, but I didn't find anyone who needed help."

Molly pushed her damp hair out of her face and whispered, "Favours? I wonder..."

Innes said, "Molly's right. Stone eggs are no use for anything. It would be much easier to do a good deed with a toolbox or a loaf of bread."

Rosalind called, "Bye-bye, have fun with your rude deed game!" The stag stepped carefully away, with the waving girl balanced on his back.

Innes said, "Let's split up, deliberately. Let's each quest in a different direction: north, south, east or west. That's the best way to guarantee I don't try to drown one of you again, or leave one of you petrifying underground, though Beth, honestly, I would have dragged you out once I'd found an egg."

"I know," said Beth. "But who did you try to drown?"

Before Innes or Molly could answer, there was a sudden flash of light.

The stag bellowed and reared up. And Rosalind fell to the ground, screaming, right under a rowan tree, which had just burst into flames.

Chapter Twenty-three

Molly, Innes, Beth and Atacama ran forward together. They grabbed an arm or a leg each, and dragged Rosalind back to the shelter of the brambles.

Molly looked up. The rowan tree was burning, fast and fierce, in the rain.

Every branch was like a sparkler on fireworks night, spitting pinpricks of fire all along its length. The red berries shone black against the brighter flames, then shrivelled and fell to the ground, faster and harder than the raindrops. The trunk was covered in roaring flames, flashing yellow and gold and orange, then white hot.

The rain fell more heavily, sizzling and steaming as it hit the burning tree, but not dampening the cursed flames.

Innes held Beth in his arms, preventing her running back to the tree. "No! You can't save it. Don't go near..."

They all watched as the beautiful living tree died in the fire.

The stag had galloped off, frightened but unburnt, and Rosalind was struggling to get away from Molly and Atacama. She kept screaming, "I can feel my tree hurting. I have to help my tree!"

Beth murmured to Innes and he let her go so she could hug her little cousin. "I know, but you can't stop it. The rain can't stop it. Nothing can stop it. The tree is cursed, Rosalind. We're all cursed. And we can't stop it."

As fire swallowed the tree whole, the twigs shrivelled and vanished, the trunk turned black and Rosalind screamed even louder. One long piercing scream of pain. Not fear, not frustration, but actual agony. The little girl sank to the ground, whimpering.

Beth whispered, "The curse burnt her too." She pointed to a bright new burn, shiny red and raw, on the little girl's throat.

Beth started to cry. "I wasn't fast enough. I didn't lift the curse fast enough to protect Rosalind. I've failed the woods and my family..."

Suddenly there were adult dryads everywhere. Uncle Pete yelling orders, the others throwing buckets of water and aiming hoses, not at the rowan tree, which was beyond help, but at the trees around it, to stop the fire spreading.

Aunt Jean picked Rosalind up and ran back towards their house. Beth said, "She'll ease the pain, but Rosalind will have a scar forever." And she sobbed into her hands.

Innes patted her shoulder. "We can't help here. Your family know what they're doing. Let's get out of their way."

They walked to the edge of the woods.

There was plenty of clear space for sitting under the trees, but they huddled close together, Atacama leaning against Innes, Molly with her arm around Beth, the toad crouched at their feet.

"Rosalind is far too young," said Innes, "to feel that pain, to bear that scar. It's not fair."

"None of it is fair," said Molly. "We've all been cursed. Not just the five of us. Rosalind is cursed too. So are these trees, and the fish in your rivers, Innes. We aren't just trying to lift the curses for ourselves. We have to lift the curses for everyone. We can't do that if we keep arguing and fighting and racing against each other. We have to lift the curses together."

"A noble sentiment," said Atacama. "But Mrs Sharpe will only lift one curse. Between us, we have five. We have to be rivals. We have to compete against each other."

"Mrs Sharpe *can* only lift one curse," said Molly. "But if we work as a team, we can lift the other four curses ourselves."

Beth stopped sobbing. The shouts and crackling behind them in the woods emphasised the silence in the air around them.

"Lift the curses ourselves?" Beth asked, quietly.

Molly nodded. "You might not have noticed all the things we've learnt this week, because you've known about curses all your lives, but on my crash-course beginner's guide to curses, I think I've learnt enough to lift most of them myself."

They all stared at her, then demanded: "How?"

"Before I tell you, we have to agree that we'll work together from now on, that we won't sabotage or attack each other any more."

Beth said, "Yes! I can't lose any more trees, I can't let anyone else I love burn and scar. And I wouldn't even have a stone egg if it wasn't for you, Molly. So yes, I'm back in the team."

Atacama said, "I agree too. We completed the farmhouse task together, but on our own we're each failing the good deed task. I'm happy to be in a team again."

They all looked at Innes.

The kelpie shook his head. "I must put my family and my rivers first. I can't waste time or energy helping anyone else. I have to do this on my own."

"That's a shame," said Molly. "Because I can see a way to lift your curse that will only succeed if someone else does it."

"What? Tell me!"

"No. Innes, you've given me very little reason to trust you. So I won't tell you – *any* of you – the ways to end your curses, unless you promise that we'll work as a team until all our curses are lifted or broken or defeated."

Beth took Molly's hand. "I'm in. I promise I will work with you until we are all free of our curses."

Atacama nodded. "I promise I will work with all of you, until we are all curse-free."

Molly looked at the toad. "I admit I don't know how to lift your curse yet, but I'll try, if you tell us what it is."

The toad stared at her, partially inflated its throat as if it was about to croak, then shook its head, turned its back on its former classmates and crawled awkwardly out of the woods.

Innes laughed. "The toad is leaving because it has no

faith in you, Molly Drummond. The toad doesn't believe that a girl who didn't even know about magic a week ago can suddenly lift curses. You hardly know anything about our world. Why would we put ourselves in your hands?"

Molly grinned. "And with all your knowledge, how's this task going for you, Innes? The stag that a four year old freed while you were arguing? The fish who's now in a horse trough swallowing a ring you accidentally crushed while trying to drown me? Or the thing with the chickens. What was the thing with the chickens, anyway? Tell us about the chickens, or promise to work with us and I'll tell you how to lift your curse using someone else's stone egg and someone else's good deed."

"But I have to use my own stone egg!"

"What? The stone egg you couldn't have stolen without Beth's rope?" She looked round at everyone. "You do realise we haven't been working separately at all, we've been helping each other the whole time, deliberately and accidentally. Innes got us into the Stone Egg Wood and I got Beth out, then Atacama got me out..."

"And you saved my life," said Innes softly. "Warning me about the moon, pulling my hoof out of the salt. Whether or not I believe you can lift our curses, I suppose I owe you for saving me." He sighed. "So yes, I promise. I promise to work in Molly's team until we are all free of our curses. NOW tell us your plan."

So she did.

Chapter Twenty-four

Molly smiled. “I’ve picked up a few clues about lifting curses from Mrs Sharpe’s workshop.”

She heard a new noise above the shouts and the crackling, and turned to look. Crows were swooping up and down in the pillar of smoke from the burning tree. One crow in the centre was diving and pirouetting and crying out in happiness.

“Curse-hatched,” whispered Beth.

“If we work together, they won’t be dancing next October,” said Molly. “Because the clue to lifting Beth’s curse was in one of Pete’s answers to the homework questions. Remember he said there are still descendants of Meg Widdershins living locally? If we can find them and ask one of them to forgive the trees, that should lift the curse. If they enjoy these woods, like most locals do, they should be delighted to help.”

Beth frowned, then nodded. “That’s worth trying.” She glanced up at the increasing number of crows above the tree, which was collapsing into a pile of charcoal.

Molly said, "Atacama, when you were cursed, your attacker stole something from you, but you can replace it yourself. You lost your riddle, but you still have the answer, don't you?"

"Yes," said the sphinx.

"So why not come up with another riddle for that answer? I know you can invent riddles, because you riddled Beth and Innes for me in the tattie field. Write your own new riddle and neutralise the curse."

Atacama flicked his tail. "But isn't that cheating?"

Molly shrugged. "Cursing you when you were just doing your job was really underhand, so I think finding a creative way round the curse is completely fair enough."

The dryads behind them were leaving because the fire had burnt out and the other trees were now safe. The screeching of the crows seemed even louder.

Molly lowered her voice and everyone leaned in closer. "We'll have to be a bit sneaky to lift Innes's curse. It was Atacama who gave me the idea, saying that in fairy tales if you do a good deed for someone, they owe you a favour. So, let's do a good deed for the fairy who cursed your dad, Innes, then in return ask her to lift the curse."

Innes looked at her. "That's actually a smart idea. But she won't let a kelpie near enough to do a good deed."

Molly nodded. "That's why you need someone else to lift your curse. One of us can use our stone egg to help her and ask the favour. It should probably be me, so I can charge my stone egg with a good deed. Then after we've lifted your three curses, I'll ask Mrs Sharpe to lift mine."

"Ha!" said Innes. "So this is still about you winning, about you getting the prize."

"No, it's about all of us getting our curses lifted. It's about not leaving anyone out."

"I think it's a great plan. Four great plans," said Beth. "But we can't stay here because..." She pointed upwards. "The crows have spotted us!"

The cursed-hatched crows were no longer swooping above the destroyed tree. They were flying in a loose circle over the field nearest the edge of the woods, whirling closer and closer to where the four teammates were sitting.

"They don't know we're planning to lift all the curses ourselves," whispered Atacama.

"But they do know we stole their stone eggs," said Molly.

One of the crows flapped down to the ground, landed, then walked towards them with jerky steps.

Then the rest swooped down. All the crows started to stride towards the edge of the woods, their sharp black beaks jabbing and stabbing the air as they advanced.

Molly and her friends stood up and took a few paces backwards.

"Let's get to my house," said Beth. "We can lock ourselves in."

"Then we'll be trapped inside," objected Innes.

They looked at hundreds of crows silently marching towards them.

Beth shouted, "We'll be *safe* inside! Run!"

They ran.

They slammed the front door behind them, followed Beth into a large living room, ran to the nearest window and looked out at an army of crows. The black birds were standing still and silent, staring at the dryads' house.

"What's going on?" asked Uncle Pete.

"Just a few crows," said Beth. "Nothing to worry about."

"But no one should go outside just now," said Innes.

"Shut all the doors and windows, and light a fire in the fireplace to close off the chimney," added Atacama.

Beth ran round the house, slamming doors and windows, while Uncle Pete knelt down to build a fire.

Molly said, "What about the toad, out there with all the crows?"

"The toad coped fine with the crow attack at Cut Rigg Farm," said Atacama.

"Anyway," said Innes, "the toad decided not to be part of our team."

Aunt Jean looked in from the kitchen. Behind her, lots of adult dryads were cleaning up after their fire-fighting operation. "Is everything alright?"

"Crow trouble," said Pete. "Those crows who dance in the smoke every year."

"They're curse-hatched crows," said Beth, "kept alive by the energy of curses. They're sort of part of our homework. Don't let the crows in and don't go out."

As Jean turned away, Beth asked, "How's Rosalind?"

"Asleep. I cooled the burn and gave her a herbal infusion to help her sleep. It hurts, but she'll recover. We all do. The trees don't."

Beth said, "Our homework should stop the trees ever burning again. Come on, up to my room." Beth led the others upstairs, but Molly knelt down by Uncle Pete as he fanned the fire.

"Excuse me, can you tell me who Meg Widdershins' closest descendants are?"

He frowned, then said, "The closest local one would be Doreen Drummond."

Molly's breath caught in her throat.

Uncle Pete continued, "I believe there are family down south as well. But none of the Drummonds are witches nowadays. I doubt they even know about the connection. Humans aren't usually proud of burnt witches in their family tree, so they don't pass the story on to their children and grandchildren."

Molly dragged in a deep breath of smoky air. "I can see how that would happen. The family, not knowing... about a witch ancestor... It would be a shock, wouldn't it? A nasty surprise. Not something anyone would want to hear." She sighed. "Thank you for telling me."

Uncle Pete nodded. "How long do you think these crows will be outside? I want to check on my own trees. They must be nervous after the fire."

"We'll try to get rid of them soon..."

"I'll have a cup of tea, then." He stood up and left the room.

Molly stared into the fire, watching the tiny cheerful flames. She heard voices throughout the house. The deep rumbling of adult voices in the kitchen, the gentle murmur of her friends upstairs.

Were they her friends? Would they still be her friends once they found out what Uncle Pete had told her?

The flames in front of her were taller and fiercer already.

She stood and walked to the window. She saw hundreds of crows, standing still like sentries in the fading evening light. But one crow was strutting and preening, showing off in front of the others. A crow with a flaming orange sheen on its right wing. That must be the dryads' curse-hatched. The crow born from the curse cast by Molly's own ancestor. How could she possibly admit that to Beth?

Perhaps she shouldn't admit it now. Perhaps she should keep quiet until after they'd lifted a few other curses. Perhaps that would be easier, and safer.

Or perhaps not speaking up now would mean the others never trusted her again.

She walked slowly to the stairs and climbed up even more slowly.

She found a door with 'Beth's Room' painted on it. Each letter was formed from a different kind of flower. Molly didn't recognise most of the flowers, just the bluebells of the B and the roses of the R.

"You'd think I'd know more about flowers and herbs, if I've got a witch in the family," she muttered.

She pushed the door open.

Atacama was curled on the bed, Beth was sitting on a beanbag and Innes was looking out the window.

She heard the kelpie say, "Let's hope Molly's smart ideas work by remote control, because we're stuck here."

"No, we aren't," said Beth. "We just have to find a way past the crows. And that's not impossible. Nothing is impossible, according to Molly anyway."

This feels impossible, thought Molly. Then she took a deep breath.

They all turned round, smiling at her, pleased to see her.

"Beth, I need to tell you something, so please don't yell or throw things at me until I've finished. Ok?"

"Of course. What is it?"

"I just asked your Uncle Pete about Meg Widdershins' family. So we could lift your curse."

"Oh, thanks. I was going to ask later, once we'd decided whose curse we're tackling first."

"Yours has to come first, Beth. Because... because I've just found out that... Meg Widdershins, Margaret Wilkie, was my great-great-great... however many greats... grandmother. I'm her descendant."

Beth leapt up and walked towards Molly. "What? YOU? You're the witch's spawn? You cursed my wood? You scarred Rosalind? You burnt that tree to death?"

Suddenly Innes was standing between them, holding up his hands, blocking Beth's way. "Hold on, Beth, let her finish."

"*I* didn't burn anyone! But apparently Aunt Doreen is her closest living descendant around here. So anyone she's descended from, my grandad was also descended from... and my dad... and me. So that means I'm also..."

Beth was staring at her. Fists clenched, teeth gritted, tears sliding down her cheeks.

"But Beth, this could make it easier. If you ask me to forgive the woods in her name, maybe I can lift the curse. And that's one curse gone before we even get past the crows."

Beth shook her head. "But the trees didn't do anything wrong. I refuse to ask you to forgive them, when they didn't do anything wrong. *You're* the evil magical witch. You're the one who should be asking forgiveness."

"I'm not a witch. I can't do magic."

"Yes, you can. You can transform into a hare, all on your own. That's magic."

"I'm just manipulating my curse. I'm not a witch, I didn't curse your woods, and I know the trees weren't at fault. But my ancestor blamed them, so if you ask me to forgive—"

"I'm not asking you for anything! Get out!"

Atacama said, "Beth, you liked the idea of asking the witch's descendants when Molly first suggested it. You'd have had to say the same to them."

"But that wouldn't be a friend, in my bedroom. Someone I trusted and liked. If you are a witch, with Widdershins blood in your veins, I don't want to ask your forgiveness and I don't want to be in your stupid poxy curse-lifting team. Get out!"

"You made a promise," said Innes.

"So?"

"Promises are harder to break safely than curses. So, keep your promise."

"The promise feels heavier than the curse. But I suppose... alright. Out of the way, kelpie, so I can see the witch properly."

Innes glanced at Molly and she nodded to him. So he moved out of the way. But not very far out of the way.

Beth and Molly stood in the centre of the bedroom, staring at each other.

Beth sighed. "Ok, witch-girl. Let's make this sound good." She held her hands out in front of her and spoke in a low voice. "All hail tricksy descendant of Meg Widdershins, deceiving scion of the Wilkie bloodline. Molly Drummond, will you accept that the trees of this wood did not hold ill will to your ancestor, will you... will you forgive the trees and the wood and the spirits within for the death by long, slow, painful, entirely deserved burning of your ancestor, and will you lift the curse that is killing our trees and scarring our family? Please."

Molly nodded.

"You have to say it," whispered Innes.

Atacama added, "Say it in the proper form. Not just 'ok.'"

Molly spoke very slowly, hunting for words that sounded important and old-fashioned. "As the descendant

of Margaret Wilkie, also known as Meg Widdershins, I acknowledge that the wood, the trees and the dryads did my ancestor no deliberate harm and were not to blame for the brutal sentence carried out by the humans of the town." She held her hands out in front of her and slowly raised them up, aware that she looked daft, but feeling that she needed a theatrical gesture to accompany her theatrical words. "I hereby forgive the trees, the wood and the dryads within for any indirect involvement in the horrid and probably undeserved death of Meg Widdershins. I hereby lift the curse that falls on this wood in October every year."

There was an uneasy silence.

Then Molly said, "Em… did that work?"

Beth shrugged. "I don't feel any different. It just sounded like we were doing bad Shakespeare. So that was totally pointless. All I've achieved is realising that I can't trust any humans, ever. So get out, hare-girl, and take your own chances with those crows."

Molly sighed. "I'm sorry, I really thought that would work. Maybe it won't be possible to lift any curses without Mrs Sharpe after all."

Innes said, "It was a good idea, Molly. Maybe it has worked, but we won't know until next October, when a tree either burns or doesn't burn."

"We can know right now," said Atacama. "Look outside."

They crowded round the window. The crow that had been strutting and preening in front of the others was now flat on the ground, its beak open and its wings slack. The glow of the flame etched on its wing was slowly fading.

"The curse-hatched is dead, so the curse must be dead too," said the sphinx. "Beth, your curse is lifted. Your trees are safe."

Chapter Twenty-five

Beth stepped back from the window, sat hard on the bed and put her head in her hands.

Innes threw his arms around Molly and gave her a violent hug. "Well done witch-girl! That was brilliant! Can you lift mine as easily?"

Molly pushed him away. "If you think that was easy, for me or for Beth, you weren't paying attention."

"It wasn't easy," said Beth, "but it *worked*!" She leapt up and hugged Molly too. "You really didn't know? About being a witch?"

"I'm not a witch. I don't know any magic, so I'm not a witch. But that's not what's important. What's important is that we can't lift Innes's curse or my curse while we're stuck in your bedroom. We could lift Atacama's in here, but at some point, we're going to have to get past those crows."

Atacama said, "Let's solve the riddle of the crows first, before we consider my riddle. Because they don't look like they're leaving..."

They peered out of the window again. Hundreds of

crows were standing, heads lowered, gazing at the dead crow. Then, at the same moment, they all raised their heads and stared at the house again.

Molly closed the curtain. "Are they just at the front or all the way round the house?"

"I checked from every window when we got upstairs," said Beth. "There was a complete circle, three crows deep."

Innes said, "We could distract them and sneak past..."

Atacama snorted. "Distract them? With what? Singing? Dancing? Puppets? Shiny things? They're crows, not magpies!"

Innes shrugged. "We could tunnel out..."

Beth shook her head. "Not through my trees' roots."

Molly said, "We stole eggs from them while they were asleep. Could we get out when they sleep tonight?"

Innes shook his head. "I don't think they'll all sleep at once. They'll post sentries."

Molly frowned. "So could we—"

They heard a sudden sharp creak.

Molly jumped, but Beth said, "It's just someone coming up our creaky stairs."

Atacama whispered, "Beth, don't tell your family that the curse is lifted. I think it would be dangerous, for us and for Mrs Sharpe, if Corbie discovers that we're trying to get rid of all the curses rather than just waiting for Mrs Sharpe to lift one. So don't tell anyone yet."

Beth nodded as Aunt Jean opened the bedroom door.

"Beth, dear, we need to talk about those crows.

The rest of the family want to check on their trees, but we're all stuck indoors. Could you do your homework with the crows somewhere else?"

Beth shook her head. "The crows are trying to stop us lifting the curses. So we have to get rid of them or get past them if we're going to finish Mrs Sharpe's workshop."

Aunt Jean sighed. "Can we help? Would Aggie think that was cheating?"

"You could help with advice," said Molly. "How did you get Rosalind to sleep?"

"A herbal infusion. Many of the herbs in this wood have a strong sedative effect, and I keep a stock of them in the kitchen."

Molly smiled. "So let's make all those crows sleepy."

"How?" asked Innes. "Crows won't sip a mug of herbal tea."

Molly said, "We could bake cakes, soak them in the herbal brew, then throw crumbs out the window, so the crows eat them... Would that work, Jean?"

Beth's aunt nodded. "You'd need lots of cake and a big pot of herbs, and if it's part of your course, you should do the preparation yourself. But yes, it could work."

Atacama said, "We'll need a good reason for chucking the crumbs out, so the crows aren't suspicious."

"Let's burn the cakes," said Beth, "as if they'd been baked by Rosalind."

Aunt Jean said, "The infusion will need time to soak in, then dry, so you'll all have to stay the night. Which is no bad thing, because you look exhausted. You can give the crows sleep-inducing crumbs if they're still there in the morning."

Molly suddenly realised they'd been up all last night building a farm, and all day today stealing stone eggs and failing to do good deeds. She yawned, setting off a Mexican wave of yawns from everyone else.

Jean laughed. "I'll find quilts for everyone. Then once your cakes are in the oven, I'll show you how to make the sleeping brew."

Soon Beth had Innes weighing flour and Molly beating eggs. Atacama was busy batting cake cases into place on a tray with his front paws, but Molly noticed he was also muttering under his breath.

Innes whispered, "He's trying to find his new riddle. That was a good idea too!"

Once the fairy cakes were in the oven, Beth put a big black pan of water onto the stove to heat, and called for her Aunt Jean.

"You'll need to chop these finely," Jean pulled handfuls of fresh flowering herbs from a rack above the dresser, "and grind these into a paste," she pulled another handful of herbs from a shelf. Then she placed three sharp knives and a mortar and pestle on the table.

Molly took her stone egg out of her pocket. "Perhaps we should grind with this, because these are the eggs those crows hatch from."

Jean smiled. "You have a natural sense of how magic

operates. So, cut that pile, grind this pile, put them all in at once and simmer for exactly thirteen minutes. You can soak the fairy cakes once it's cool."

Jean tidied up the cake-mix-splattered kitchen, while Molly ground and the others chopped.

Molly looked down at the stone egg in her hand and felt how right it was to escape from the curse-hatched crows using their own un-hatched egg as a tool. Then she looked up at Jean, who was rinsing spoons at the sink.

"Excuse me, Jean. What makes a person a witch? And what exactly is a witch?"

"There are good witches and bad witches, in both senses. Witches who use their power for good, and witches who use their power for evil. But also witches who are good at what they do, skilled and powerful magic users, and witches who just dabble. Witches tend to be human: people who can recognise the magic around them, then learn methods to manipulate that magic. You now know about the magic around you, because you've met a handful of beings who are born to magic. But most beings like us have only our own limited magic, we don't usually access any other kinds. Kelpies shift shape; dryads speak to trees. We *are* magic, but we don't *do* magic. Witches, on the other hand, can harness all the different magics around them, if they can find someone to teach them."

"So a person can't be *born* a witch?" asked Molly.

Jean started scrubbing the mixing bowls. "No one is born a witch. The knowledge is often passed down in families, and a heightened ability to harness magic can be inherited too. But no one becomes a witch without both the ability to work with magic, then the effort of learning specific spells. No one is born a functioning witch. Why do you ask? Do you want to be a witch?"

"No! I just wondered what Mrs Sharpe was."

"Aggie Sharpe is good and powerful, but also aging and tired. So you just want to learn how to lift a curse?"

"Yes."

"Then don't look for more. Don't chase more spells than you can handle, Molly."

Molly nodded and added another handful of fragrant leaves to the paste she was grinding.

Soon the herbs were in the water, the deliberately burnt cakes were out of the oven, and the infusion had simmered for exactly thirteen minutes. Aunt Jean made everyone sandwiches while they waited for the infusion to cool.

They spent a messy half hour dipping each cake in the mixture, letting it soak up lots of liquid, then sitting it on a rack to dry. Beth wrote a sign:

Dryads! Do not eat!
Danger of Dozing...

Then everyone went upstairs to bed.

Beth lent Molly pyjamas, and they all lay down: Beth in her bed, Molly in a sleeping bag on the floor nearby,

Atacama and Innes on the other side of the room in a pile of quilts and pillows.

When Beth put the light out, they could hear nothing, no creaking stairs, no wind in the trees. No crows. But they knew the birds were out there, standing still, staring at the house.

Molly whispered, "I'm not a witch, Beth. You heard what Jean said. Just because I'm related to a witch, doesn't make me a witch."

"No. Ok. You're not a witch. So what are you, Molly Drummond?"

"I'm a girl who can run fast. But once my curse is lifted, I'll go home to Edinburgh and school, and I'll be an ordinary girl again..."

Chapter Twenty-six

"So, why are we throwing crumbs out of all the windows?" asked Innes.

"Don't you remember why we baked and soaked all those cakes last night?" Molly was lacing up her trainers.

"Yes, *I* know why we're doing it, but we don't want the crows to know," said Innes. "So what reason can we give them for throwing crumbs out of all the windows?"

"The cakes are burnt, so we're getting rid of them," said Beth. "Rosalind often throws crumbs out for the birds..."

"Out of *every* window? At the same time?"

"The crows will be hungry," said Beth. "They've been there all night. If we give them a vaguely convincing reason to peck at the crumbs, they'll eat them, then fall asleep before they can think, 'Huh? Why did those kids do that?'"

"You hope."

"I hope."

"It doesn't need to be every window," said Atacama calmly. "Just the middle window on each side of the house. If we argue loudly about the quality of the cakes at each window, then throw them out at the same time, most crows will only see it happening from the window they're facing."

"There are four of us and four outside walls," said Innes. "We'll have to argue with ourselves."

Beth laughed. "You're perfectly capable of starting an argument in an empty room, Innes Milne, so that should be easy enough."

They all stood up. Dressed and washed and ready for a day of curse lifting.

"I'll do the kitchen window," said Beth. "Atacama and Innes, take the two different walls of the living room, and Molly, you'll have to take the downstairs loo. Throw your crumbs when I signal with the dinner bell. Ok?"

Molly carried her bowl of burnt cake crumbs into the bathroom. The only way to reach the small window was to climb onto the toilet. So she put the bowl on the sink, closed the toilet lid, and clambered up, one foot on the lid, one on the cistern behind. She leant over, wobbling slightly, to pick up the bowl.

But as she stood straight again and stretched to see out of the window, her left foot slipped off the cistern and landed on the handle.

The toilet started to flush under her feet, splashing and groaning as if the plumbing was under too much pressure.

Molly pulled herself up so she was crouching on the vibrating cistern, and looked outside at three curved lines of stern black crows.

“These are rubbish cakes,” Molly said loudly. “I’ll flush them down the toilet.”

“No,” she squeaked in a high voice. “I baked those cakes all by myself! Don’t put them down the toilet, it’s not polite to the cakes.”

“But no one can *eat* them,” Molly replied in her own voice, feeling very silly, perched on a toilet, arguing with herself. “They’re burnt. They’re horrid. I’m going to put them down the loo.”

“NO! That’s a waste. The birds and the slugs and the earie-wigs will eat them.”

Molly could hear voices in other rooms, in a variety of high and low pitches, all arguing about cakes. She raised her voice very slightly. “No! Don’t grab!”

“NO! They’re mine!”

She was wondering how much longer she had to keep this up, when she heard the bell.

Molly pushed the window open, lifted the bowl and shouted, “Ok, the slugs and the earie-wigs can have your cakes, because even the toilet is making funny noises at the idea of eating them!”

She flung the crumbs in a wide arc towards the crows. “That’s what I think of your baking!”

The swinging throw knocked her off balance and she slipped off the cistern, her foot hitting the flush again, then fell onto the tiled floor. The bowl landed upside down on top of her, scattering crumbs in her hair, while the toilet flushed loudly beside her.

She sighed and clambered back up to look out the tiny window.

The crows were rushing forward, arguing and cackling, croaking and pecking, eating up all the crumbs.

Molly smiled.

Then the crows returned to their posts in the still silent creepy circle.

She held her breath. A couple of crows preened their feathers. A couple of crows clacked their beaks. But all the crows stood upright, wide awake, staring at the house.

Molly shivered. Would they be trapped here forever?

Then she saw a crow yawn. And another. One crow fell forward onto its beak, then another fell sideways, knocking over a whole row of yawning black crows, like a line of unspotted dominoes.

Suddenly all the crows were yawning and drooping and falling. Then they were all flat on the ground, snoring.

Molly grinned and stepped carefully off the cistern, avoiding the flush, then down from the toilet onto the tiles.

Rosalind was standing in the bathroom doorway, her dark hair loose and fluffy, and a bandage round her throat. "Why were you feeding cakes to earie-wigs? And why were you standing on the toilet? You're meant to sit on the toilet!"

Molly smiled. "Beth will tell you the story later. How's your throat this morning?"

"Sore, but not as sore as the place in my tummy where the tree used to live." Rosalind pointed to her chest, to her heart.

"I'm sorry," said Molly. "But that horrible fire won't burn any more of your trees."

Rosalind grinned up at her. "Promise?"

"I promise."

Molly stepped round the little girl and ran to the kitchen.

Everyone else was already there and no one else was covered in crumbs. Beth asked, "Why did you flush?"

Innes asked, "Twice?"

Molly laughed and flicked crumbs out of her fringe. "Are they all asleep?"

Atacama nodded. "Every single one."

Beth opened the door. "Ok. Molly and I will cycle through town and meet the two of you at the gorse village, then we can try to persuade the fairy who cursed Innes's dad to accept a good deed."

Atacama said, "No, wait, look..."

A larger crow was swooping down through the trees. They all flinched as it shrieked in anger at the sight of the sleeping crows, the same reverberating shriek they'd heard when the crows attacked them at Cut Rigg Farm.

The crow landed and started kicking at the crows on the ground. But it was kicking with black leather boots, not clawed feet. When it landed, it had shifted into the tall man they'd seen talking to Mrs Sharpe.

"Get up, lazy bones," he shouted. "Get up!"

But the crows didn't move.

"We have to get out of here now," whispered Beth, "before Corbie notices us."

Innes nodded. "Atacama, get to the fairy village by yourself, I'll bring the girls faster than they can cycle." As the sphinx slunk off into the woods, Innes stepped outside and shifted into his horse self.

Molly backed off, remembering teeth on her shoulder and tentacles around her waist.

"Come on," said Beth, climbing onto the white horse.

Corbie was flapping round in the distance, his black coat flicking, yelling at the snoring crows. He was flying up as a crow, then crashing back down as a human.

Molly realised that every time he became a crow, he was slightly bigger, with a wider wingspan.

"Come on, Molly!"

"But kelpies in their horse form are dangerous to people!"

"Not Innes, not today." Beth held out her hand. "He really believes you can lift his curse, so he needs to keep you alive. You'll be safer than any human has ever been on a kelpie's back. *Come on!*"

Molly reached up and Beth hauled her onto Innes's back. They rode out of the woods, away from the sleeping crows.

Molly balanced nervously on the back of the predatory horse who'd nearly drowned her yesterday. He galloped through fields and along farm tracks around the edge of Craigvenie.

She'd only been on a horse twice before, at friends' pony-themed birthday parties, when the horses walked slowly in a circle. But she held tight to Innes's mane and Beth held tight to her waist, so once she got used to the rhythm, she felt quite secure.

Beth shouted, "There are no birds following us. Perhaps Corbie didn't see us leaving."

Innes didn't slow down until he was trotting along a rutted road leading to a field at the base of a low hill. He leapt over the fence into the grassy field.

Beth let go of Molly's waist. "Jump down!"

Molly slid off, landing on her hands and knees. Beth jumped down beside her.

Innes was standing beside her too. "You've not done that before, have you?" He smiled. "I've not had a human on my back before either. It's usually too risky."

"You've not had a human on your back before?" Molly stood up. "So you've never actually lured someone onto your back, dragged them into the water and eaten them?"

"Of course not! I'm more of a pizza person, to be honest. And we're part of the community here, so we don't eat our neighbours. If I wanted to try a traditional kelpie diet, I'd go somewhere else. Did you really think I made a habit of eating people?"

"When I asked before, you didn't give me a straight answer."

"He's embarrassed," said Beth. "He thinks he's denying his kelpie heritage."

Atacama loped up beside them.

"There you are, slow paws!" said Innes. "I beat you again, even with these two heavy lumps on my back."

The sphinx smiled. "So you've had plenty of time to come up with a plan, then. What are your tactics?"

Innes frowned and looked round. "Em..."

Beth pointed to the base of the hill. "The fairy village is in that clump of gorse bushes, by the side of that burn. It's a small settlement, with a couple of dozen fairy families. They need to be close to Craigvenie so they can gather flower seeds and petals from the gardens."

Innes said, "We need to watch the gorse village, find our fairy target, then work out how to help her with Molly's egg."

Beth said, "You won't be able to go near her as a boy or as a horse. She'd recognise you as a kelpie, and get suspicious."

"Obviously. I'll hide in the burn as a pike."

They agreed to split up round the field and watch different exits from the fairy village. Molly asked, "Who exactly are we looking for?"

"The heather fairy," said Innes. "She'll probably be dressed in purple. Let's watch for an hour, then meet at the furthest corner of the field to discuss what we do next."

Innes crept over to the burn, Beth sauntered quite openly up to a clump of birch trees and sat with her back to the tallest one, and Atacama climbed up a much bigger tree nearer the fence and lay along a branch like a shadowy leopard.

Molly shifted into a hare and lolloped past the gorse bushes to the moorland slope above, where she lay flat on the ground.

From her low vantage point she could see little round houses, with tiny doors and no windows, hanging from the bottom branches of the gorse bushes. They were woven out of dried grass and rosebay willowherb stems.

Birds cheeped in the trees and the burn shooshed below her. Then the fairy village came to life.

Tiny people stepped or flew out of the houses.

Molly watched, entranced. This week she'd seen a boy turn into a horse, answered a sphinx's riddles, watched a girl vanish into a tree, and spoken to a legless dragon. But this was the most magical thing yet.

She lay in her hare's form, staring at the fairies.

They weren't glittery and they weren't all young and pretty. There were wrinkly fairies and plump fairies, male fairies and female fairies, and they were wearing sensible clothes made of grass and petals, rather than tight-fitting silk party dresses. But they were definitely fairies. They had wings and they would be small enough to stand on Molly's human hand. And they were chatting, in quiet high-pitched conversations that a passerby might mistake for birdsong.

Then a fairy dressed in muted purple and green, who was neither young nor old, flew out of the village towards the hillside, with a couple of folded sacks over her shoulder.

Molly lay still as the tiny fairy fluttered past. She saw

the fairy land further up the hill and start to fill one sack with faded papery heather blossoms.

The hare watched as the fairy harvested. Nothing else moved except a few insects buzzing about. Molly saw how long it took the fairy to fill the bottom of the sack and realised this would be a slow job. It would be a couple of hours before the fairy even started on the second sack.

Molly wondered if she could offer to speed things up.

She could hold the sack open. She could pick the flowers. But how could she use the stone egg? She wondered if any of the others could see the heather fairy at work, and if they had any bright egg-shaped ideas.

Molly sat up slowly, raising her ears, then her shoulders, trying not to startle the fairy.

The fairy looked up, nodded at the hare and went back to her harvest.

Molly looked down at the village and the field. She was the only one with a close-up view of the heather fairy and her long task. She'd better go and report back to the others.

Then out of the corner of her wide eye, Molly saw a sudden movement. She crouched down again, quivering with fear.

That wasn't just a movement. It was a shape, a colour.

A sharp red movement.

There was a fox. On the hillside. Stalking her.

Chapter Twenty-seven

Molly's hare heart was racing with fear. This wasn't a daft dog who would chase her because she was moving and snap at her for fun.

This was a fox. A predator. An animal that lived by killing. A hunter that might have killed hares before.

What should she do? Should she stay still? Maybe it hadn't seen her, maybe it wasn't stalking her.

But she couldn't see it. That sudden flash of red had moved into the blind spot behind her.

The fox – if it was a fox, if it was there – was directly behind her. With a clear line to her spine, her neck and her skull.

Molly shivered. She couldn't just lie still, feeling so small, so defenceless, so vulnerable. She had to know if there really was a fox.

She moved her head, very slightly, just enough to see behind her.

And there it was.

A fox.

Just metres away.

Molly didn't see the rust-coloured fur or the wide bushy tail. She only saw the narrow squinting eyes, the naked lips stretched back over vicious yellow teeth.

And she saw the fox dart forward.

So she ran.

The fox ran after her.

Molly had no idea how fast a fox could run, but she hoped it wasn't as fast as a greyhound.

She dodged about the hillside. She jumped over the fairy and the sacks, the blast of moving air from her speed blowing the loose sack away. She leapt over the heather, twisting and turning around the hillside.

But the fox wasn't wrong-footed by her changes of direction. This fox knew how to chase a hare. It anticipated her every move. It didn't have to run as far as her, because it was able to cut the corners of her zigzag escape.

Molly kept running, but she tried to think too. The first thing she thought was that the fairy would need help keeping her sacks on the ground if it got windy, which wasn't a handy thought right now.

The next thing she thought was that heather was harder to run on than grass, which wasn't useful either.

Then she thought that what she needed was a boundary, because the fox wanted to eat a hare, not a girl.

She angled down the hillside onto the flatter field, then aimed for the rutted road, hoping that the fields on the other side were owned by a different farmer. Now she had a plan, she ran in a straight line, trusting that her pure speed on grass would beat the fox.

She sprinted towards the fence, using every scrap of power and speed she had, then she laid her ears back and jumped between the middle two strands of wire.

Molly crashed onto the gritty road in her jeans and fleece.

She turned to see a fox snarling at her from the other side of the fence.

"Ha!" she called. "I'm not your lunch today. Go and eat snails..."

The fox ran off, looking glossy and beautiful now that it was a fraction of her size.

Then Molly became aware of a metallic roar.

She looked along the road and saw a red tractor rattling towards her. She shook her head. If she kept using roads as boundaries, she was going to get run over.

She climbed the fence, hoping the farmer hadn't seen her rolling about, and walked towards their rendezvous point in the far corner of the field. She wasn't a hare any more, but her heart was still beating far too fast.

Atacama was already there. "I saw the end of that chase," he said. "I was too far away to help, but you had the speed and the boundary, so I knew you'd be alright. Molly, you have to be more careful about when you use your hare form. I know it's convenient, but if you're not in control of changing back it's too dangerous."

Molly nodded, still shaking.

Beth and Innes appeared too: Beth calm and smiling, Innes with wet hair and a scowl.

"Those fairies are so irritating," he said. "All that singing and chattering and washing their petticoats in the burn. I couldn't see the heather fairy from where I was anyway."

"I saw her," said Molly, her voice a bit wobbly. She sat down and Atacama sat beside her, his heavy furry warmth leaning into her, calming her.

She said, more firmly, "I saw the heather fairy, she's on the other side of the village, gathering heather blossom. And I have an idea about how to help her, because when I was being chased by a fox—"

"A fox!" interrupted Beth. "Are you alright?"

"I'm not being torn apart and eaten, and I didn't get run over by the tractor I threw myself under, so yes, I'm fine. Anyway, while I was running from the fox, I leapt past the fairy and the gust of air lifted her sack. I wonder if we could offer to weigh her sack down with a stone egg, so it doesn't get blown away?"

"Blown away by what?" asked Innes. "It's not windy today. Or are you planning to ask lots of hares to run up and down the hill?"

"It was just an idea!"

"It's a good idea," said Beth. "We just need to create some wind."

"Can you change the weather, Beth?" asked Molly.

Beth shook her head. "We'd need a strong witch for that. But branches move in the wind, so I wonder if I could

do it the other way round. Start the branches moving and see if that causes a breeze."

"Not now though," said Atacama, tipping his head as if he was listening. "The laundresses and harvesters are heading back to the fairy village. When they return to work after lunch, Beth can build a breeze and Molly can offer the fairy help."

Molly could hear faint noises from the bushes: birdsong conversations and tiny bursts of laughter from groups of fairies on their way home. Then she noticed Atacama was silently moving his lips again.

"Are you trying to write your riddle?"

The sphinx nodded.

"Can we help?" offered Innes.

"No. You can't help without the answer, and I can't tell anyone the answer, because if I did, no door I guard would ever be secure."

Molly said, "I'll be back to a non-magical life in the city soon, Atacama, so you can tell me your answer."

Beth said, "You can tell all of us. I'll promise never to tell anyone else the answer, if that would help."

Atacama smiled. "If you all made that promise, I could trust the whole team with the answer."

So they all promised never to tell anyone else the answer to Atacama's riddle, then the sphinx whispered, "The answer is… a clock."

Innes said, "What about: *My face shows the time, but no emotions.*"

"Too simple," said Atacama. "I don't want anyone

unworthy to get past me. Using the word 'time' is too obvious."

"We could use 'face', but not 'time'," suggested Molly. "What about: *You can say what you like to my face, but I won't show any emotion.*"

"That's good," said Beth. "And clocks have hands, so what about: *Talk to the hand.*"

Atacama snorted. "I can't use naff out-of-date slang in an elegant riddle."

"The hands work though," said Innes. "What about: *I move my hands all day, but I never make anything.*"

"But a clock does make something," Molly pointed out. "It makes a noise. Tick tock tick tock."

Innes nodded. "Alright, try this: *I move my hands all day, but I never wave with them or pick my nose with them or...*"

Beth said suddenly, "Tock! Talk! That could be a pun. Riddles have puns, don't they?"

Atacama nodded.

Beth grinned. "So: *I tock all day, but I never tell you anything.*"

"But clocks tell the time!" said Innes. "And anyway, 'tock' and 'talk' are spelt differently."

"Yes, but sphinxes speak their riddles," said Beth. "They don't write them—"

"Shhh!" said Atacama. "Wait! I almost have it." The sphinx lay down and put his paws over his face.

After a few silent minutes, he sat up and said solemnly:

I tock all day, but I never say hello;
I move my hands all day, but I never wave goodbye;
You can say what you like to me,
but my face will never show any emotion.
What am I?

"Wow," said Beth. "Well done, Atacama!"

"We all wrote it," said Atacama, "as a team, working to lift all our curses."

Molly nodded. "But is your curse really lifted, I wonder?"

"I don't know." Atacama had a wide smile on his long face. "But I have a riddle and I have an answer, so I can go home and tell my family I'm a real sphinx again."

"Now it's just you and me, hare-girl," said Innes. "We're the only ones still cursed. And we can lift both curses by helping one fairy..."

So Beth walked over to the birch trees and chatted to them about breezes. Atacama and Innes found hiding places with a view of the hillside. And Molly took the stone egg out of her pocket and waited.

She could hear the faint noises from the village change from chattering to clattering. Were they finishing lunch? Then three fairies fluttered out towards the water. She looked up the hill and saw Atacama nod to her. That meant the heather fairy was returning to her harvest.

Molly glanced over at the trees and saw branches moving back and forth, more like oars pushing through water than branches blown by the wind. But they must have affected the surrounding air, because Beth's purple hair was whipping around her face.

Then Molly felt her own hair ruffled by a breeze. It was time to head for the hillside.

She didn't want to surprise or scare the fairy, so she walked slowly towards the clump of heather the fairy had been harvesting earlier and said gently, "Hello. I saw you working and I felt the wind getting up, so I wondered if I could help you?"

There was no answer. She took one step closer and saw a sack blown up against the heather stems, but no fairy.

Molly crouched down and touched the sack.

"Leave that alone!" The fairy flew out of the heather and yelled at her in a shrill voice. "That's a whole morning's work. Leave it alone!"

Molly looked over at the waving trees sending billowing gusts of air in their direction. The sack lifted off the ground for a moment.

"You won't want to lose it then, so I wondered if I could help. I could place this stone egg," she held it out, the browns and coppers glowing in the afternoon sunlight, "on the sack to stop it blowing away. Then I could collect the egg later, when you've finished."

"No," said the fairy. "I harvest heather every October and I have my own methods to ensure I don't lose blossoms to the weather. So, no thanks, strange human child."

Molly frowned. "Are you sure? I mean, the wind is *getting really strong now*," she said loudly, and the branches whipped around more vigorously.

"I'm sure. Now, go away, interfering child, before your huge feet or that heavy egg crush me and my flowers."

"But..." Molly couldn't think of anything else to say.

Suddenly the sack moved, jerked fast backwards.

Molly and the fairy watched as the sack was dragged away by...

A toad.

Not just a toad. *The* toad. The very familiar sand-coloured toad.

The fairy yelled, "Oy! That's mine!"

But the toad gripped the corner of the sack in its wide mouth and almost ran on its splayed legs, moving rapidly downhill through the heather.

"Bring that back, toad, it's not yours!" shouted Molly.

The toad turned, stared at her, then crawled away again at speed, dragging the open sack, scattering frail purple blossoms.

The fairy shouted, "Help! Stop! Flower thief! Help!"

Molly grinned. "*Now* you want help? Ok!" She weighed the stone egg in her hand, then rolled it down the hill.

The egg clipped the back of the toad's legs, knocking its feet out from under it. As the toad fell, it dropped the sack.

Molly ran over and crouched down. She picked up the egg and the sack, and whispered, "Are you ok?"

The toad croaked once and limped off dramatically.

Molly walked back up the slope. "Here." She laid the

tiny sack on the ground beside the fairy. "You shouted for help and I helped, with my handy stone egg."

The fairy fluttered over her sack. "You may be a strange interfering child, but I'm lucky you were here. Who would have thought a stone egg could foil a blossom thief?"

Molly smiled. "It certainly wasn't on my list of useful things to do with a stone egg."

"Thank you for doing me a favour. I owe you a favour in return. So, one wish only, and don't ask for pots of gold or handsome princes. I deal in purely practical things: heather honey, herbal shampoo..."

Molly spoke carefully. "I have one favour I could ask you. A fairy in your village put a curse on the father of a friend of mine, a kelpie. I'm sure she regrets it now because the curse has already killed countless innocent water creatures. So could you please ask the fairy to lift the curse? As a favour to me, after I stopped that thieving toad?"

The fairy stared at her. "That fairy was me."

"Was it? I couldn't be sure."

"Did you come here today to ask me to lift the curse?"

Molly nodded.

The fairy folded her arms. "Did you ask that toad to steal my blossom?"

"No! That was a surprise to me as well!"

The fairy sighed. "You might be right – about the regret. I meant the curse at the time and I refused to lift it when that murderous kelpie demanded, threatened and begged. But a lot of time has passed since then, a lot of salt has flowed under the bridges, and a lot of innocent water-dwellers have died. Perhaps I do regret it, a little, now."

She thought for a while, rolling a heather blossom between her hands, then said, "I do not forgive the loss of my children, but I no longer wish the Spey kelpie and his family cursed. I lift my curse, willingly and freely." She raised her hands and the tiny heather blossom blew towards the burn.

"There. It's done. Now, leave me alone with my harvest."

Molly said, "Thank you so much."

The fairy started to pick up the spilled petals.

Molly asked, "Can I help with that?"

The fairy replied quietly, "No, leave me now. I wish to think of the lost children, in peace."

Molly nodded. "Thank you again, and I wish you a successful harvest." She walked slowly away.

The wind had died down and the silver birches were steady and still. Innes, Beth and Atacama stood under them, waiting for Molly.

"So? What happened?" Innes's voice was hoarse with tension.

"Our wind idea didn't work. But the toad had a better plan."

"We saw that. But what did she say, Molly, what did she do?"

"She was suspicious of my motives, but she regrets the curse now, and when I asked for the favour, it gave her a chance to reconsider. So, Innes… she lifted your father's curse!"

Innes sat down, speechless for once.

"Do you want to search for a dead crow, to be sure?" asked Beth.

"No, I know the curse has gone. I feel safer and calmer… and less like I have salt in my veins, needling me and poisoning me and… scaring me all the time. Thank you, Molly. Thank you for saving all of us from our curses. Now, let's lift your curse too."

Chapter Twenty-eight

"We can walk at human pace back to Skene Mains," said Innes. "There's no rush, we're not racing each other. Mrs Sharpe probably won't want to see us until she's closed the shop anyway."

As they walked along the farm tracks round the town, Molly rolled her stone egg between her hands. "It doesn't feel any different, now it's charged with a good deed. Will Mrs Sharpe be able to tell?"

Beth pulled out her stone egg. "I've just realised that my egg was probably charged with a good deed yesterday, because you gave it to me." She smiled at Molly.

"But we were meant to charge our own eggs, not each other's," said Atacama. "And only Molly has managed that."

When they reached the next crossroads, Innes said, "I don't think we should approach the farm through the front gate, in case the crows are awake and searching for us."

Beth nodded. "Let's go over the hill and in the back way."

They scrambled up a hillside. From the top, Molly could

see fields and rivers and woods all around, with the town and distilleries behind her and the mountains far ahead. "How do we get to Skene Mains from here?"

Innes pointed. "Down this hill, ford that river, walk respectfully through the fields of Mrs Sharpe's neighbours, then we'll come in by her tattie fields. Though I'm not howking any tatties this afternoon."

When they reached the shallow river, Innes dived in, changing into a long sharp-snouted pike, and swam over, scrambling out wet and laughing at the other side.

Atacama picked his way across carefully, using a network of stepping stones, shaking his paws in irritation when they got wet.

Beth and Molly just splashed over.

When they clambered up the steep riverbank and pulled themselves onto the flatter farmland beyond, Molly saw a figure standing by a barbed-wire fence. She wondered whether it was the neighbouring farmer, and whether they should ask permission to cross his fields.

Then Molly realised that most farmers don't wear long black coats.

Long black *fringed* coats.

Molly hadn't seen Corbie's face at the farm, but she wasn't surprised to find that it was pale and pointed, with a sharp nose and sharp chin.

Corbie held a dead crow in his right hand, its bony legs grasped in his fist, its limp body dangling down. He flicked his hand and the crow's wings opened, revealing a glistening white crystalline image on the feathers of its right wing.

Innes said, "Salt. That's salt. That's my curse-hatched! I really am free."

"You're not free, boy. Not yet. You will not get past me until I have what I want."

"What do you want?" Innes asked, warily.

"You've killed three of my curse-hatched family this week: the birds bearing the wyrm, the flame and the salt on their wings. All strong crows, hatched from strong curses. Now they're dead, because you selfish children can't accept that you're cursed. I won't let you reduce my army any more. I won't let you use those stolen stone eggs to lift more curses. Give me back all the eggs *now* or you will be sorry."

"Really? There are four of us and only one of you," said Innes. "We have hooves and claws on our side. And your army is dead or snoring."

"Your puny hooves and claws don't scare me. I have gathered immense power from all the suffering caused, over many generations, by my ancient curse!"

The dead crow fell to the ground, as Corbie's hands and arms became wings.

Suddenly he was taller than any of them, a massive black-feathered monster looming over them.

The giant crow shrieked his violently loud call, then whirled round, his wings knocking them all to the ground, and snapped at the barbed-wire fence behind him.

The fencepost broke in two as Corbie's beak closed

round it, and when his head jerked up, the whole fence ripped out of the earth, like the field was being unzipped.

The bird whipped the barbed wire over their heads and flung it in a heap behind them, blocking their way to the river.

Then the crow shrank back down to the man.

"I'm not afraid of your claws and hooves. My claws and beak are bigger and stronger, and my wings carry me through the air faster than your hooves can gallop. You cannot escape me, so give me the eggs, or I will peck out your eyes and open up your guts. *All* the stone eggs, *now*!"

Innes stood up and held his hands out to Beth and Molly, pulling them to their feet. Atacama leapt back onto his paws beside them.

Innes shrugged. "He's right. I can't outrun a beast with that wingspan. It would be like racing an aeroplane."

Beth said, "But if we give him the eggs, we can't keep our promise to Molly."

"In a choice between a promise to a human and my own life, I know what I choose."

Beth gasped. "Innes! That's so... selfish!"

Innes smiled. "Mr Corbie, sir, I need to persuade my companions of the wisdom of your offer. May we have a moment to chat?"

"Of course."

Innes led them away from Corbie, to stand in a huddle near the wrecked barbed-wire fence.

Molly said, "I understand if—"

Beth broke in, "Innes! You'll never persuade me to betray a friend!"

"Glad to hear it," he murmured. "I'm not going to try. Now shut up and listen to me. We're going to debate this loudly. But we're also going to talk quietly, to come up with a plan. Because he's right. We can't escape. Not all four of us. And we can't give up Molly's chance to be free of her curse. So if we can't escape and we can't give him what he wants, then we'll just have to fight him and defeat him."

Beth nodded, then said loudly, "You horrible treacherous kelpie!"

Innes laughed. "You shouldn't be surprised! I'm a shape-changer, and we change our minds and our loyalties easily too..." Then he whispered. "So what skills and powers do we have that could defeat a giant bird?"

Beth said, "I can't do anything. There are no trees close enough and it would take too long to awaken the life in those old fenceposts."

"I could attack him as a horse," said Innes, "and give you all time to escape. But..."

"But you wouldn't win, would you?" said Molly gently.

"No. I wouldn't. The three of you might reach safety though."

"I could help," offered Atacama. "Hooves and claws together. But even then..."

Beth said loudly, "I can't believe you're siding with him, you sleekit cat!" Then she whispered, "No, Atacama. We're a team. We're not leaving anyone behind. There must be a way to defeat him and his huge beak."

Molly said shrilly, "How can you do this to me, Innes?" Then she looked over at Corbie. "The beak is only dangerous if he can catch us. And he can't do that if he can't fly."

Corbie yelled over, "Hurry up, kelpie. If you haven't persuaded them yet—"

"Five more minutes and you will have your eggs, sir." Innes lowered his voice, "Ok, Molly. How do we stop him flying?"

Molly smiled. "We clip his wings. I've held Aunt Doreen's hens while she clips their wings. You cut the ends of the primary flight feathers on one wing, so the bird doesn't have the balance or lift to fly. Anyone got scissors, or a knife?"

They all shook their heads.

Innes called to Corbie, "That was a vote, sir, but we're doing a recount."

Molly said, "What's the sharpest thing anyone has with them?"

Innes grinned. "My pike's teeth."

Molly nodded. "Right. Here's what we do. Beth and Atacama, distract Corbie with the other stone eggs. Innes, change into a pike and I'll aim your jaws at the feathers I want you to bite off."

Innes took two eggs out of his pocket and gave them to Beth. "My egg and Atacama's egg." He turned to Molly. "I can only survive for a couple of minutes out of the water as a pike. So please be fast."

They all faced Corbie.

"We've agreed," called Beth. "Here are your eggs."

She laid them on the ground. The purple egg, the river-blue egg and the pearly egg.

As Corbie stepped forward, Atacama patted the eggs with his paw and rolled them into the tangle of barbed wire.

Corbie screeched in frustration, shifted into his massive crow form and flapped over to peck at the wire.

Molly whispered, "Now!"

Innes shifted into a long fish, shining silver-green on the ground. Molly grabbed him and ran towards the giant bird. "Beth, Atacama, pull the wing open!"

Beth grabbed the edge of the wing to drag it away from the crow's body, and they all saw the gleaming scales of a mermaid's tail on his outstretched feathers.

The crow screamed and started to turn round, almost knocking them to the ground again.

"Hold on!" called Molly.

She held the pike's jaws up to the middle of the first long feather. The fish bit down and the tip of the feather fell to the ground.

She aimed the live fish clippers at the next long feather and it fell too.

"I can't hold on," yelled Beth, as she was flung about at the end of the wing.

Atacama leapt onto the wing to weigh it down. Together they wrestled with the wing as Innes bit and broke more feathers.

The crow whirled round again, but they all tried to stay behind the wing, out of reach of the jabbing beak.

Innes bit another feather.

"Just one more!" called Molly.

Beth screamed as the wing jerked violently. She was flung towards the barbed wire and landed just centimetres from its jagged spikes.

Molly aimed the pike and he bit again, but with less strength this time. The black feather bent but didn't break.

The crow wheeled round even faster, dislodging the sphinx. A wall of hard feathers struck Molly in the chest. She fell to the ground and dropped Innes, who flapped feebly in the grass.

Molly looked up to see the crow's long sharp beak stabbing towards her face.

She rolled away, and the beak pierced the earth beside her.

Molly desperately wanted to become a hare, to run and hide from this terrifying bird. But she saw Atacama scramble onto Corbie's wing again, and Beth stagger up to grab the bent feather. So she struggled to her feet, seized Innes by his long scaly tail, ducked under the bird's stabbing beak and round to the wing again, to the last of the longest flight feathers. She held the fish more firmly and pointed his jaws at the bent feather. "Just bite once more, Innes, then you can breathe."

He bit and the feather broke.

Molly laid him on the ground. Innes shifted into a boy, gasping and coughing.

"We have to run, now!" yelled Molly.

"I can't run, not yet..." groaned Innes.

As the crow spun towards them again, she and Beth grabbed the kelpie's arms and dragged him over the empty fencepost holes and into the field, Atacama running beside them.

They heard screams behind them.

The crow was flapping, but his shortened wing wouldn't take his weight. He couldn't fly.

"Stop dragging me!" Innes protested. "Let me find my legs."

They stopped as the bird shrieked in frustration and tried to waddle after them.

The crow shifted into the man. His coat was ripped, with one lopsided sleeve. "You treacherous children! Don't you dare lift any more curses!"

"We're going to lift Molly's curse," yelled Beth. "And you can't stop us!"

Innes shifted into the tall white horse. Molly and Beth climbed up and they cantered towards Mrs Sharpe's farm, Atacama running alongside them.

Corbie screamed, "You might be pleased with your petty week of curse lifting, but when my crows wake up, when I call on the power who maintains the curses, and when my feathers grow back, then I will make your lives such a misery you will wish you were still cursed!"

"I am still cursed," said Molly.

Beth laughed. "Not for long."

Chapter Twenty-nine

Mrs Sharpe was sorting tatties behind the shop when they ran into the farmyard. She frowned. "I didn't expect you to arrive together, in a dead heat. I can still only lift one curse."

"That's fine," said Beth. "Most of our curses are lifted already. Molly is the only one still cursed."

Mrs Sharpe glanced upwards. "Do the crows know you've been lifting curses on your own?"

"Yes," said Atacama. "We just clipped Corbie's wings by the river."

The witch smiled. "Oh dear. He'll be angry. But if I only lift one curse myself, he'll have to accept I stuck to our agreement, so my farm will be safe. Well done all of you for using everything you learnt so effectively and for outwitting the curse-hatched."

Molly jumped off Innes, landed on her feet and held her egg out to Mrs Sharpe. "Here's my stone egg. I used it to save a fairy's sack of heather blossoms."

"Let's do this properly," said Mrs Sharpe. "In the barn, where it all began."

They pushed open the red door.

And there, squatting on the front desk, was the toad.

Molly groaned. "How could we forget the toad? The toad can't carry an egg, so it had no chance of completing the final task. But the toad helped us dig the tatties, the toad built the outhouse, and the toad saved our good deed at the fairy village." She slumped down on the nearest chair. "We don't even know what the toad's curse is. It could be as life-threatening as yours, Innes. But my curse doesn't have to be life-threatening. I can cope. When I'm a hare I'm faster than you, Innes, and better camouflaged than you, Atacama. I can survive my curse, if I have to."

She stood up again. "Mrs Sharpe, I wonder if—"

Beth grabbed her arm. "Molly, don't do this!"

Innes said, "No, Molly! You've worked so hard to lift your own curse. Don't give it away."

"Molly, this is a big decision," said Atacama. "Think about it carefully."

"I've thought about it and I know what I have to do. Mrs Sharpe, here's a stone egg, charged with a good deed. Please use it to lift the toad's curse."

Mrs Sharpe took the egg carefully in both hands. It glowed, shining and coppery, in her fingers. "There is a good deed in here, a slightly tricksy one by the feel of it, but the egg is also charged with teamwork and an unbroken promise. It has power. Stand back, everyone."

Molly, Beth, Innes and Atacama moved to the other side of the room.

Mrs Sharpe put her left hand gently on the toad and held her right hand out with the egg standing upright on her palm. She muttered seven soft sing-song words and threw the egg on the floor.

The egg shattered and a puff of silvery-blue dust rose into the air.

And the large sandy toad turned into a small green frog.

Innes said, "A frog, cursed to turn into a toad? That's not a very ambitious curse."

"Wait," said Mrs Sharpe. "It's not finished."

The frog turned into a weasel.

The weasel turned into a ginger cat.

The ginger cat turned into a swan, which flapped off the desk onto the floor.

The swan turned into a goat.

And the goat turned into a boy. A tall dark-skinned boy in a sand-coloured cloak, with his bare scalp covered in raw scrapes and small cuts, like he had been badly shaved.

He bowed towards Molly. "Thank you. That was a very kind thing to do. I hope you never regret it. And my apologies to you, brave sphinx, for any trouble I caused you. It was a pleasure to dig and build and steal with all of you this week. Farewell."

The boy vanished inside a pillar of golden sand, which whirled out of the open door, past the frowning sphinx.

"Who was that?" asked Innes.

"I have no idea," said Mrs Sharpe, "but he was under an incredibly complex curse, with lots of layers. It needed all the power of your good deed, your teamwork and your promise to break it. Whoever cursed him must be an extremely powerful magic user." She glanced around nervously. "I'm definitely not holding any more of these workshops. It's becoming far too complicated and risky."

"You don't have to hold any more for us," said Molly. "You've taught us everything we need to know about curses already."

Mrs Sharpe smiled. "Don't assume you know everything. That was just an introduction to the world of curses." She left the classroom, still looking about anxiously.

Molly turned to Atacama. "I'm sorry I seem to have un-cursed the person who cursed you."

"That's ok. I think you made the right decision."

"I *know* you made the right decision," said Innes. "Now you're still a part-time hare, I'm going to start training and build up my speed so I can beat you in a fair race."

"Racing isn't the priority," said Beth. "We must search for other ways to lift your curse."

"In the meantime, we should create a map of local boundaries," suggested Atacama, "to help you shift back more easily and safely."

"Those are all great plans," said Molly. "You all think about training and searching and mapping. I'm going out to stretch my legs."

Molly went outside.

She growled softly. She felt the familiar warmth up her spine. She watched as her pale hands became long paws.

Her vision widened and her hearing got more sensitive.

She became herself. Her hare self.

And she ran.

As she leapt into the nearest field and sprinted across the grass, she heard, in the far distance, the croaking of crows waking up. But she didn't care. Not today.

Molly knew exactly why she was running like this. This incredible fast leaping flight, feet barely touching the ground. She was running because it was the right thing to do, the best thing to do, the only thing to do, with these legs, and this blood pumping through her veins.

She felt she could run like this forever.

She didn't feel cursed at all.

Desperate to find out what happens next?

Read on for a sneak preview of

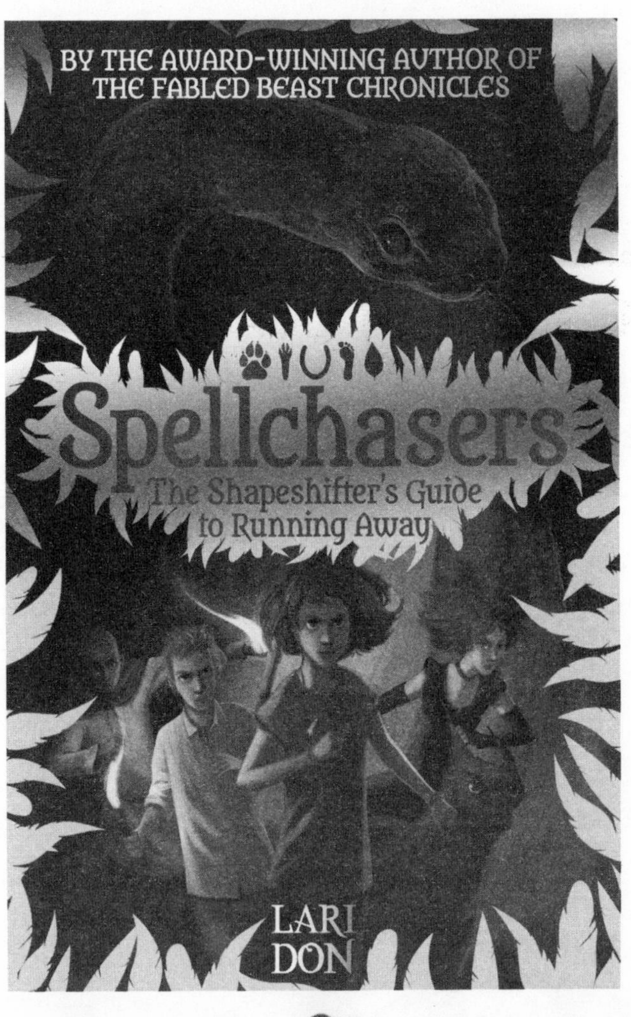

Chapter One

Molly's curse got worse early on Sunday morning.

Molly expected to become human as she leapt through the air.

She expected to beat Innes to the finish line as a hare, change shape when she crossed the stone wall into Aunt Doreen's garden, and crash-land on the ground as a girl.

That's what always happened.

She always beat her friend Innes when he challenged her to a race. She always controlled her curse by crossing a boundary and becoming human again, just in time to accept his grudging congratulations.

But this time, when she landed on the ground, she didn't fall and bash her knees. This time she stayed on all four feet. All four paws.

She was over the wall, over the boundary, and she was still a hare. Still small, vulnerable, defenceless. Still unable to speak.

Innes thumped down on his heavy hooves, shapeshifted from white horse to blond boy, then said, "Well done.

how you do it. I was the
...til you arrived. You weigh less
...ou don't even train, and you still
...time. It's not... fair. But, obviously,

...answer.

...d. "Why have you shifted back to a hare already? ...o you want another race? I will beat you eventually, but I'm not giving it another go until I've had one of your great-aunt's biscuits. So bounce over the wall and become a girl again. You're easier to chat to when you can talk back."

Molly turned and jumped over the wall, hoping it had been some kind of magical blip, hoping the rules of her curse would work as usual this time.

She landed in the field neatly and elegantly. She was still a hare.

Over the past week, Molly had got used to being a part-time hare. She enjoyed the speed and the strength of her long hare legs and she loved beating Innes in races. But she didn't want to be a full-time hare.

She'd learnt to manipulate this curse, with the help of her new friends. She'd discovered that, as well as becoming a hare unwillingly when she heard a dog bark or growl, she could choose to shift from human to hare by growling like a dog herself. She also knew that she always shifted back from hare to human when she crossed the boundary between one owner's land and the next: a garden wall, a playground fence, a road cutting between two farms. So why wasn't it working now?

She leapt the wall again, still enjoying the power of her legs and the precision of her senses, but also starting to feel trapped inside this small fragile shape. She landed, on all four paws. She was still a hare.

Molly looked down at her delicate brown paws, wondering if she'd ever see her pale human fingers again.

Innes was frowning. "Why are you still a hare?" He crouched down and placed a hand gently on her back.

With his warm palm on her spine, Molly was suddenly aware of her fast jerky breathing. Stuck inside this hare body, she was beginning to panic.

"Calm down, Molly. We'll work this out. Maybe this wall is, I don't know, broken or something. Let's try other boundaries..."

Innes wrapped his hands round her ribcage, about to pick her up. Molly flicked her ears in annoyance, slid out of his grasp and sprinted across her aunt's garden. She leapt over the hens' wire run, hurdled the wooden fence into Mr Buchan's weeds, then jumped a white wall onto the Websters' lawn.

She was still a hare.

She swerved round in a tight circle and ran back. Over the wall, over the fence, round the confused chickens, back to Innes.

"So walls don't work and fences don't work," he said, "even though they worked yesterday. We'll have to change you back another way." He paused. "I shift by thinking about the shape I want to be. Why don't you try that?"

Molly's ears drooped. Innes changed easily because he was a kelpie, a born shapeshifter, able to become human or horse or fish or monster at will. She'd been cursed to change from human to hare, so she had much less control over her shapeshifting.

"I know," said Innes, "it's probably not as easy for you. But see if it works."

Molly closed her wide-vision eyes and pictured herself. Her girl-self. The self she had been every minute of every day until Mr Crottel had cursed her. She saw freckles and fingers. She saw bruised knees, poky elbows and short brown hair. She focused and she wished and she hoped.

And it made no difference at all. She was still a hare.

"This is beyond us," said Innes. "Let's ask Mrs Sharpe. She knows a lot more than she taught us on that curse-lifting workshop. If your curse has got worse somehow, she'll know what to do. Let's go to Skene Mains farm."

They walked down the narrow garden, through the back door into the kitchen, then crept through the bright cottage. As Innes opened the front door, Molly heard her Aunt Doreen call from the living room. "I'm off to Elgin soon to get some messages, so I'll not be back until teatime. See you later, Molly."

Innes muttered, "Alright. Bye," and dashed through the front door before Molly's aunt could identify his voice.

He shut the door and put Molly down on the pavement

in front of the row of houses between the distillery and the town.

He asked, "Would you rather go to Skene Mains the long way round town on your own paws, or the short way through town under my coat?"

She pointed her nose at the hills.

He grinned. "Race you?"

She shook her ears.

He sighed. "Ok. I know. On unfamiliar territory you have to be sensible, you have to keep an eye out for predators and snares. No race then; let's just meet at the farm gates. I bet I'll get there before you!"

Molly sprinted over the empty road, then into the fields that would take her in a long curve round the town of Craigvenie to Mrs Sharpe's farm.

As Molly ran at a comfortable speed, looking out for dogs, foxes and barbed wire, she realised Innes was galloping one field higher up, looking for more challenging obstacles to leap.

Each time she pushed under a gate or leapt a wall, she hoped to hit the ground with a human-sized crash. But each time, she was still a hare.

Then she ran into a grassy field and saw a moving shape to her left.

Was it a predator? A fox?

Molly dropped to the ground and lay flat, hiding her soft brown contours in the folds of the field. Then she recognised the shape.

It was a hare. Three hares. Long-legged and long-eared, like larger stronger faster rabbits. Silhouetted clearly on the grass of the field.

Molly had never met any other hares. She wondered if these hares would think she was a real hare, or only a pretend one.

She watched them.

They were grazing together, moving around each other, not too close, but clearly comfortable as a group.

They were all female. Molly wasn't sure how she knew that. But she did know it, even more clearly than she'd know whether a distant teenager in jeans and t-shirt was a boy or a girl.

These were girl hares.

So she moved towards them.

She knew they could see her. Her own vision was so wide she could see almost everything around her, except just in front of her nose and just behind her head. The hares had stopped cropping the grass. They were all standing very still.

Then the largest hare turned round to watch Molly approaching.

Was there a hare language? Molly wondered. Would she understand it?

Molly loped closer.

The other two hares turned round.

She moved even closer. Slowly. Not wanting to scare them.

But they didn't seem scared. They didn't seem suspicious or puzzled. They just stared at her.

The largest hare loped towards her. Molly tried to look friendly, with no idea what a hare would think was friendly. The hare reached Molly and stood up, showing her pale belly. Molly nodded a greeting.

The large hare punched her. Just whacked her, right on the nose. And again. And again. Punching, boxing, hitting.

Molly squealed, a noise she hadn't known she could make, and backed off.

She raised her own front paws, planning to fight back. Then she realised this hare was just defending her territory, or her babies, or her grass, or something else important to a real wild hare. Molly didn't want any of those things. Molly didn't want to fight her.

So when the hare bobbed forward to punch her again, Molly turned and ran away. She ran as fast as she could, away from the hares, towards the witch's farm, hoping with all her heart, for the first time, that she could lift this curse, and that she wouldn't have to spend her life trying to make friends with hares who punched her before even getting to know her.

She ran, knowing the only native animal in Scotland that could overtake her – a larger hare – was right behind her. But as she darted under the gate, the other hares were already nibbling grass again. Like she hadn't even been there.

Molly sprinted across the last few fields to Mrs Sharpe's farm. And she thought about grass. She'd never eaten as a hare. She'd always changed back in time to eat human food. If she was stuck as a hare, would she have to eat grass?

She stopped and looked at the grass under her paws. She bent down and sniffed the sour salad smell.

No. She wasn't hungry enough. She'd try eating grass later if she absolutely had to.

As she ran through the last field, Innes joined her, sweating from his gallop and jumps.

Molly knew that even though she was faster than Innes, she wasn't a true shapeshifter like him. He was equally at home as a horse or a boy. She wasn't really a hare. Perhaps it was time to accept that: to say goodbye to the speed and freedom of being a hare. Perhaps she really did have to find a way to lift this curse forever.

She leapt over the fence into the road, and ran between Mrs Sharpe's gateposts.

She felt an unfamiliar fizzing in her bones, tumbled forward in an uncontrolled somersault and caught a wide-angle glimpse of fur-covered paws stretching into long bony fingers. Then her vision narrowed, her hands hit the ground and her palms scraped painfully across the gravel.

Molly was a girl again.

But it had never happened like that before. She'd never seen herself shift from one shape to another; it usually happened too fast.

Molly shivered. Her curse had definitely got worse.

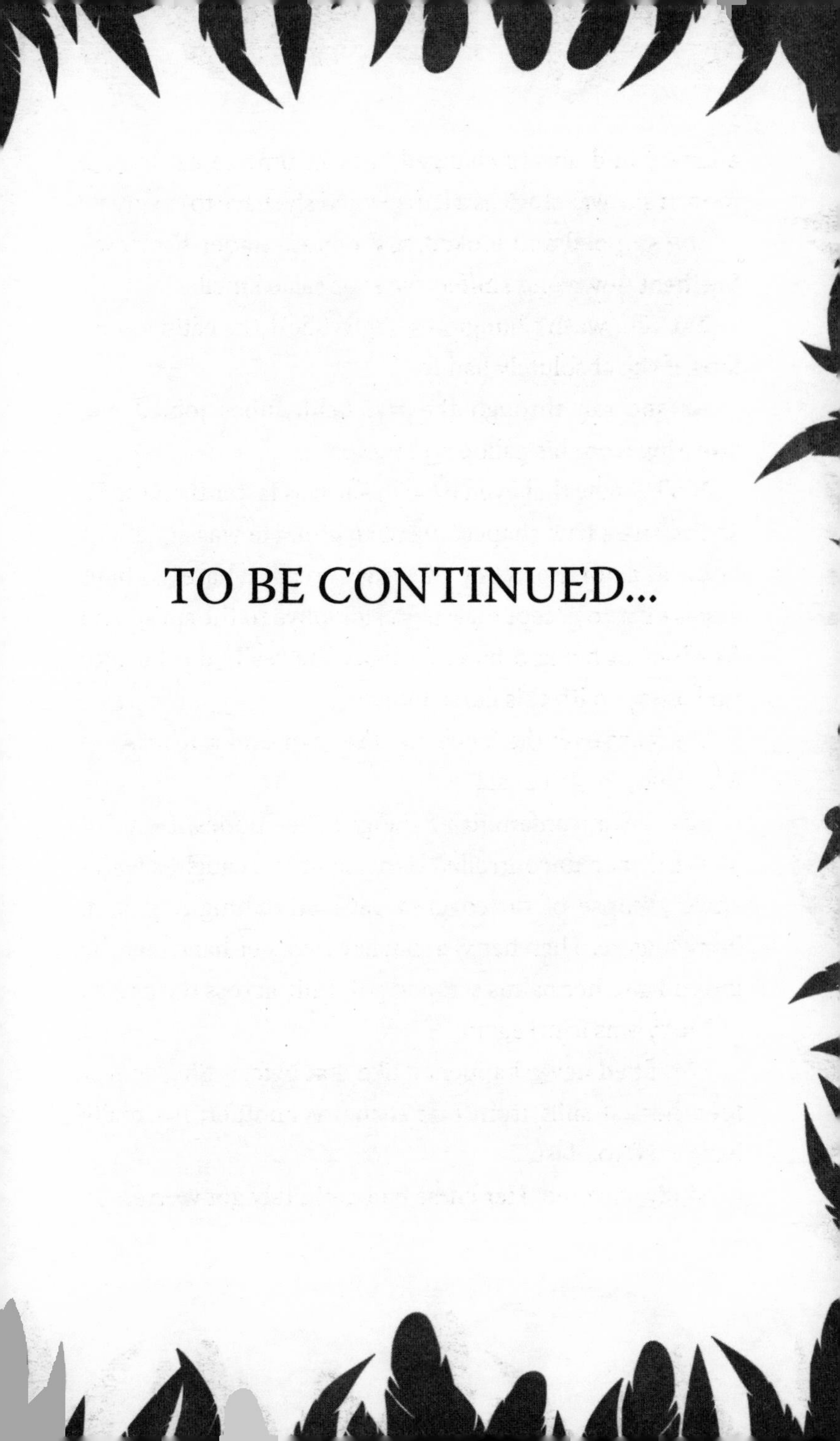

TO BE CONTINUED...

Will Molly finally break her curse?

Beth frowned. "This wouldn't have happened if you'd ever truly committed to lifting your curse."

"Like being willing to become a witch?" Molly asked.

"Given the choice between being a part-time hare or a full-time witch, I still think the cursed hare is a better option."

Molly's curse is getting stronger and more unpredictable. Can the friends bring balance to the magical world in the final thrilling instalment of the *Spellchasers* trilogy?

Also by Lari Don

FABLED BEAST CHRONICLES

It's not every day a grumpy, injured centaur appears on your doorstep. And that's just the beginning...

Helen's first aid kit comes in very handy when she meets Yann's friends – a fairy, a dragon, a phoenix, a werewolf and even a selkie – who have a habit of getting into trouble.

Together they must solve riddles, fight fauns and defeat the dangerous Master of the Maze before midwinter and the end of the world.

"*A gripping fairytale that will keep you reading past your bedtime*" Cait, age 8

Including

First Aid for Fairies and Other Fabled Beasts

WINNER OF A SCOTTISH CHILDREN'S BOOK AWARD

FABLED BEAST CHRONICLES
First Aid for Fairies
and Other Fabled Beasts
LARI DON

FABLED BEAST CHRONICLES
Wolf Notes
and
Other Musical Mishaps
LARI DON

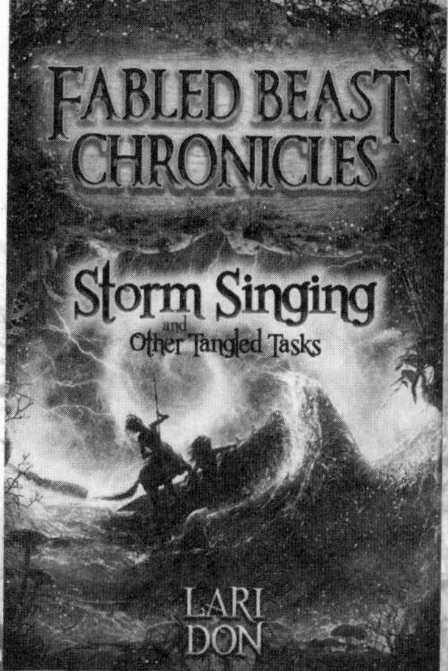
FABLED BEAST CHRONICLES
Storm Singing
and
Other Tangled Tasks
LARI DON

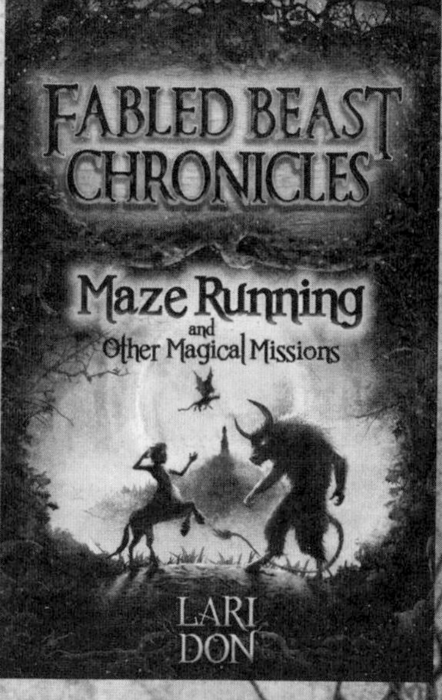
FABLED BEAST CHRONICLES
Maze Running
and
Other Magical Missions
LARI DON

LARI DON

ROCKING HORSE WAR

EMBRACE THE MAGIC.
DEFY DESTINY.

From the prize-winning author of
First Aid for Fairies and Other Fabled Beasts

EMBRACE THE MAGIC.
DEFY DESTINY.

One sunny morning the triplets disappear, leaving only a few mysterious clues behind.

Older sister Pearl sets out to find them. Her journey unfolds into an incredible and perilous adventure.

Can Pearl save her brother and sisters from the unknown fate that lies ahead?

"A mystical tale set in the Scottish Highlands in the 1920s and woven by a true storyteller..."
—Carousel

"A fast-paced, well-crafted tale of betrayal, magic and adventure."
—Bookfest